MW00451425

Greater Need

Lori Bell

This book is a work of fiction. Names, characters, places and incidents are the product of the author's imagination or are used fictitiously. Any resemblance to actual events, locales, or persons, living or dead, is coincidental.

Cover photograph by CanStock Photo

Printed by CreateSpace

ISBN 978 1795710503

DEDICATION

My heart goes out to all of you who have ever been lost
in the deafening silence and lonely pain of grief.

In loving memory of my beautiful cousin,
Abby Robke.

March 4, 1988 – December 11, 2018

Chapter 1

She nudged his bare shoulder. His back faced her. From the sound of his breathing, she knew he was asleep. "You need to go," she said to the man lying beside her in bed, in the dark.

"Hmm? She startled him awake. It was that disappointing moment of drifting off to an almost immediate sound state of rest, only to be disrupted.

"Go."

The rumpled sheet fell away from his body as he sat up. He reached blindly for his pants on the floor and he slipped into them commando. He pulled on his shirt, knowing it was likely inside-out. One at a time, he stuffed his bare feet into his shoes found conveniently paired together on the floor. No boxers. No socks. Maybe leaving those personal things behind could be a reason, or at least a justifiable excuse, for him to see her again soon.

Hunter Raine pulled up the sheet to cover her bare chest. She laid back on her pillow and closed her eyes. Sleep didn't always come easy for her.

"I'll see you again?" she heard him ask across the room, from the open doorway.

"Good night," was her response. It's what she did now to any man who wanted to get closer to her. She gave in to physical desire, but she left her heart out of it.

¥¥¥¥

Backstage at ABS NewsChannel 7 studio, in Detroit, Michigan, Hunter was already in full makeup when she plopped down in the *hair chair* — as she and everyone else simply referred to it. She looked directly into the mirror in front of her. Aggie was standing behind her. Both of her hands were gripped on the shoulders of Hunter's favorite seafoam green robe that she kept at the studio to wear during the hair and makeup ritual.

"They're telling me we have no time for an up-do today, as you're on in twenty-eight minutes." Aggie, whose own dark locks were pulled up high on top of her head in a bun that sprouted several wiry hairs, never defied orders or attempted to race the clock. She played on the safe side, always. She already had the curling wand heated on the makeshift vanity in front of them.

Hunter nodded in agreement, and stifled a yawn. Her plum lipstick would likely need a touch-up before she went live on-air, because she had already smudged it with the back of her hand. Aggie ran her fingers through Hunter's long, white-blonde locks. Her roots were dark and the contrast with platinum blonde was striking. "Late night?" Aggie looked at her overtop her dark wire-rimmed glasses and smirked.

"Sometimes I wish your husband wasn't the head of my security team," Hunter rolled her blue eyes and then blinked as the amount of mascara on her lashes felt too heavy this morning.

Aggie giggled. The two women were six months apart in age, as Aggie had reached thirty-three and Hunter was trailing behind, as she liked to state it. "The cameras showed your guest leaving close to midnight."

"So?" Hunter realized how childish she sounded. And she wondered if all of the men on her security team blabbed to their significant others. She doubted so, as Aggie was the closest thing she ever had to a best friend. And Aggie likely pried the private information out of her big, broad-shouldered man.

"On a school night?" Aggie partly teased because they were grown adults, but she didn't agree with Hunter's carelessness. "And, bringing a stranger home is seriously stupid, risky, and dangerous."

"Anything else?" Hunter pushed her.

"Was the sex good?"

"Absolutely. Christian never disappoints."

"Oh so you're seeing him? I mean, you know him?" By now, Aggie was twisting Hunter's hair around the curling wand and already had it looking close to presentable for her live morning news audience.

"You're insinuating that I'm promiscuous. And no, I'm not seeing him," Hunter clarified. "We just know what to expect from each other. Acquaintances with benefits, actually. No strings. Just doing what two God-given bodies are designed to do together."

"And then you send him home." Aggie stated as a matter of fact, like she knew the drill of Hunter's personal life. And, well, she did.

Raine to wardrobe in eight minutes, fifty seconds.

The backstage intercom blared. The voice overhead typically controlled Hunter's routine in that studio, but she really didn't mind. Sometimes she needed to be kept on task. This time, the dictatorial interruption was perfect timing. She preferred not to talk about her unwillingness to let love in again. She wouldn't watch the sunrise with anyone else. She promised herself that three years ago.

¥¥¥

Clustered studio lights were hot above them, as Hunter sat chair-to-chair, facing the widow of a Detroit police deputy. The fallen officer had only been thirty-five years old and newly promoted to a deputy when he was gunned down during a domestic violence call that led to a hostage crisis with small children involved. Hunter had done her research. This story was a year old. She was prepared to be both professional and compassionate. But this assignment was too close to home. The producer of ABS NewsChannel 7 was well aware and questioned Hunter twice about passing on this feature story before finally giving in when Hunter insisted *she could handle it because she could relate.*

The small-framed, petite woman in front of her wore a simple black pantsuit with matching Lucky Brand ballet flats on her feet. She was plain, but pretty, and well composed. The focus of this interview was going to be on the young widow's quest to keep her heroic husband's memory alive. She had spearheaded, from the ground up, a mission to raise awareness about heroin abuse. The man who killed her husband had been a dealer, and a user. He had attempted to use his own two small children as leverage that night to escape the police. When his six-year-old little boy broke free and climbed out the front window, the deputy ordered his men to hold their fire as he made a desperate attempt to rescue the boy. During that risk to bring the boy to safety, the gunman fired a shot at his own child. Anticipating that, the deputy held his fire and dove midair to shield the boy with his body. The gunman went down from a police bullet to the neck just seconds after the deputy was shot in the back, lying face down with an unharmed child beneath him on the concrete porch floor. Two men were shot dead that night. Senseless loss. Consequences of substance abuse.

"It's been one year," Hunter began as the cameras were rolling, "and you already have established a foundation in your late husband's memory to bring awareness to the dangers of heroin. The drug that you believe is solely responsible for the death of Deputy Rick Gaines." Hunter watched the woman before her come to life. She was tiny-framed, but self-assured and confident when she spoke. "Your words, countless times as you've spoken to primarily high school students in packed gymnasiums or auditoriums," which was the prime age group for which studies showed a rise in heroin use, "have been that heroin was the culprit behind a man's reckless decision to shoot and kill your husband."

The young widow nodded. "That is correct. I believe that entirely. My husband knew that too. He opened my eyes to it, as he tried to save these people on the streets every single day of his career on the police force."

"The gunman who took your husband's life also lost his life that night. Mrs. Gaines, if the murderer were still alive, would you feel the same way? Would you believe that he deserved the chance to be reformed, or perhaps on a more personal level — forgiven?"

"Yes." The deputy's widow spoke without hesitation. "Absolutely I do. Tragically, his children no longer have a father, as my baby girl was robbed of a parent as well. I am going to spend the rest of my life preaching the dangers of drugs to vulnerable, impressionable high school kids. And if only one in every few hundred truly hears me, I will have done something good and made a small difference in my husband's memory."

This time, Hunter nodded before she spoke. "What our viewers are looking at on the screen now is the website address and additional contact information for your foundation in memory of Deputy Rick Gaines, the groundwork that you have established to honor him and to save even just one, or perhaps a few, lives. Thank you for joining us today, Mrs. Gaines."

The camera panned out, and the sidebar story during the live news broadcast had come to a close. It's what Hunter Raine did best. She was the heart and soul of that news channel. She was Detroit's very own Oprah. She only had a four-minute segment for this particular story, so her focus had to be on the foundation and the widow's belief that she could change the world. She was serious, but too damn kind and nicety nice, *if anyone had asked Hunter.* The person who murdered her deputy husband was a madman who had gone after his wife and own children. Drugs or not, he was to blame. Stranger or not, Hunter was glad he was dead.

And now all of the strong feelings that pulsated through her veins during and after the live broadcast had overwhelmed her. Hunter reached for the widow's hand one final time, and thanked her for coming, just seconds before she unclipped the tiny microphone from her low-cut silk white blouse and left the floor of the main studio to seek refuge in her office.

She sat behind her desk and pulled open the top drawer. She twisted off the cap of a shiny silver flask and took a slow swig of vodka. Her hands were trembling. She closed her eyes. The tears stung. *The cameras were off now. To hell with her makeup.*

Hunter Raine, the pillar of strength, almost let herself cry but she was interrupted by an abrupt knock on her office door. She cleared her throat and spoke, "It's open."

She watched the producer of ABS News walk in. The morning broadcast had been off the air for merely minutes. He had come straight to her. Hunter's first and only thought was that Bruce Rudis, the mastermind behind Detroit's highest-rated news program for the last decade, was checking up on her. He had proven, time and again, to look out for her. He was, after all, the man who hired her. The first person in the mass communications business more than a decade ago who believed she had talent —and immediately belonged in front of the camera— even when she was fresh out of college and completely inexperienced.

"You played it safe," were his first words to her after he closed the office door behind him.

"And you expected more from me?" she asked her boss, unafraid to stand up to him, or for herself. "I had four minutes. I couldn't waste it crying about my own experience."

"It wasn't your best work," Bruce told her honestly, "but I liked your angle. You called her out on being more like Mother Teresa than the grieving widow whose world was shattered after a terrible tragedy. You focused on how she stepped up to make a difference."

"I admire her ability to forgive or make excuses for the son of a bitch who killed the man she planned to spend forever with." Hunter Raine never held back. Even before life turned her heart cold and her beliefs bitter, she spoke her mind. The man in front of her believed that was her greatest quality in the business world, along with being a natural talent.

Bruce nodded, and then found a corner of her desk to sit on. His silver hair was healthy and full all over his head for a man in his mid-sixties. Rumors of his retirement had been circling around the studio for a half dozen years, but Hunter knew he would never be ready to give up constructing newscast after newscast. He was the most integral member of their news production team. No one could handle the high pressure in that environment the way Bruce could. Hunter witnessed others try, but they had not come close to his caliber. The man sitting in front of her, atop her desk wearing a dark suit, sans a neck tie, which was his trademark, was both her mentor and a father figure.

"It's easier to forgive than to forget," Bruce told her.

"I struggle with both, actually," Hunter admitted, but she knew that would come as no surprise to anyone who understood her well.

"No kidding," Bruce chuckled, and Hunter grinned at him. "You did alright out there," he spoke in his serious, complimentary way. "You've been through your share of pure hell, and it's no one's business in the public eye to know the damage it's done."

Hunter swallowed hard the lump that rose in her throat. "I'm doing okay, Bruce. No need to fret about me. See this face?" Her forced smile was wide, her eyes were bright, and her makeup accented her striking features.

"Beautiful. But underneath this flawless exterior of yours, this perfection that you want everyone to perceive — is pain. That heart of yours is raw. I could see the hurt in your eyes today during the broadcast. That was too personal for you. Still." He paused before he spoke what was truly on his mind, "Hunter, the world just keeps turning but you're not moving on."

Her wide smile faded, and her bright eyes instantly teared over. "Good thing everyone else cannot read me as well as you can."

Chapter 2

It was one of those nights when sleep didn't come easy. She knew why her mind was reeling. She blamed the live interview with the police deputy's widow today. Those four measly minutes had brought it all back to the forefront of her mind. And then there were those words that were stuck on replay in her head. *The world just keeps turning but you're not moving on.*

Hunter threw back the covers on her four-poster bed, sans a canopy at the top of those tall and big-around vertical columns. She planted her bare feet on the hardwood floor and walked out of her bedroom. The house was huge. Entirely too much space for her, but she loved it anyway. She earned it. Her successful career had put her in a place where she wanted for nothing — materialistic. At the end of the long hallway, she reached the top of the stairs. She made her way down. A few dimmed lights, which she kept on all night long, illuminated her way through the immense living room and into the kitchen. She stood in front of the open stainless steel refrigerator door. It was the middle of the night. That already uncorked bottle of wine would have to wait. She took a glass off the counter and filled it with crushed ice from the refrigerator's dispenser. She added water, and just as she stepped back the glass slipped out of her grip and shattered on the floor at her feet. The shock of cold iced water on her bare toes was enough to completely wake her up and keep her that way for hours.

"Damn it!" she yelled out, alone, in that house.

She backed cautiously away from the broken glass on the stonewashed wide-tiled floor at her feet. Her first thought was to grab a handful of paper towels — or a mop. And then her cell phone on the charger, sitting on the countertop of the island in the center of the kitchen behind her, rang. The tone startled her. *Who would be calling at two o'clock in the morning?* She shouldn't have been surprised when the caller identification told her it was her security team. Hunter answered on the second ring, expecting to hear the voice of Jay Marks, the man in charge of her safety — and the husband of her best friend and hairstylist, Aggie.

"Hunter? This is Sebastian, in for Jay Marks tonight. We heard a crash."

She paused. *Shouldn't she be the first to know if there was a change, or an addition to, her security team?* "I don't know you," she said. "Put Jay Marks on the line."

"Not happening, ma'am. He's tending to a family emergency. I'm what you get tonight. And from the calm of your voice, I assume all is well. So what was the crash? I'll need to report it."

"Just me being clumsy. You can add a broken glass to your report. Now, if you don't mind, I have a mess to clean up, Mr. Sebastian."

"It's Sebastian. Just Sebastian, as in my first name." Hunter rolled her eyes. "You know I can see you, right? That eye roll you just did. Yeah, I saw it." *Hunter tried not to react. The camera feed couldn't pick up an embarrassed, flushed face, could it?*

"Of course you can see me," she began. "The cameras in all the rooms of my house, with the exception of the bedrooms and bathrooms, were just brilliant for me to agree to."

"Just keeping you safe, ma'am."

"Knock off the ma'am bullshit. I'm thirty-two years old, hardly ancient." She heard him clear his throat on the opposite end of the phone, or possibly he concealed a chuckle under his breath.

"Certainly, Ms. Raine."

"Hunter."

"Right, Hunter. I apologize for the interruption to your private time." Hunter looked down at what she had worn to bed. A pale pink tank top, no bra, and a matching pair of lacy bikini panties. It didn't bother her in the least. She often forgot about the cameras, but it mattered none as she was entirely comfortable with her body — and couldn't have cared less who was looking.

"You're just doing your job," she told him.

"If that's all then, good night. I'm just a phone call, or a loud crash, away if you need my attention."

She almost giggled. "Thank you, Sebastian."

"Bash."

"I'm sorry, what?"

"People call me Bash."

¥¥¥

That house in the suburbs of Detroit, and the security system —complete with live cameras and a team to protect her around the clock— was nonexistent until three years ago when Hunter's entire world was shaken and altered in ways she could never have imagined. She was the face of Detroit's morning news, then anchoring the first hour of the newscast as well as featuring her own interview segment. She was admired by thousands, and stalked by one.

The police were alerted each time she received a crazed letter from the same fan. And then there were the three times she caught him following her in public. She lived in a high-rise apartment building in a spacious mid-century modern community in the historic Lafayette Park neighborhood of downtown Detroit. She had always felt safe there, as she had not lived alone, and each time she came and went from the building, an armed guard —undercover as a doorman— greeted her.

It was the night they had no warning that would forever stir panic deep in her soul. She and her fiancé, Aaron Cooper had taken two steps outside of their apartment building. They were dressed to the nines with plans of attending a Christmas party at ABS studios. He was a cameraman whom Hunter had met early in her career. She called him Cooper. They were friends first — as neither one of them gave in to the mutual attraction they both later confessed to initially harboring. They were both attached to other people, but their friendship grew for an entire year and a half before they shared their first kiss and connected on a physical level, leaving neither of them wanting to live the rest of their lives without the other. Until that tragic night when a despicable human being who had been following and stalking her for several months wanted to take away the man Hunter Raine planned to marry on New Year's Eve. It was two days away from Christmas and just a little over a week before their wedding day when Cooper was gunned down and died on the front doorstep of their high-rise building. In that horrific moment, when Cooper collapsed, the armed guard pulled his gun to protect Hunter and himself. And then, merely ten feet away, the stalker also went down.

Hunter laid on the ground beside the love of her life, her hand covering the bullet wound as the bleeding profusely worsened.

Stay with me!

Somebody call an ambulance!

We have to save him!

Oh my God! Cooper! Don't leave me. Don't you dare end us. Please, honey, please. Just fight. Hold on...

The armed guard's coat was wadded up beneath his fisted hands as he knelt on the ground beside one of the most striking, deeply in-love couples he had ever laid eyes on in his fifty-five years of life. He applied direct pressure to the wound until the paramedics arrived. Aaron Cooper didn't live to make it onto a stretcher and into the ambulance. He died that night on a typically bustling downtown sidewalk where people stopped in crowds to stare in shock, disbelief and sadness. Everyone knew who they were. Their story. *The beautiful television anchor and her fiancé.* They were always photographed out on the town together. Their love was storybook.

His last sporadic, breathless words to her were, *"I... love... you... forever."*

Hunter sobbed overtop his chest. Her white gown and matching fur shawl were saturated in her lover's blood. *"I will never love anyone else. You're it for me. You're taking my heart with you, Cooper."*

The play-by-play of that night was reeling through her mind again, as she lay back in her king-size four-poster bed all alone. That wasn't the way it was supposed to end. Her career, her fame, had taken the man she loved from her. Another person out of his mind had fired one shot with the intent to kill. He too was fatally shot that night. Not that revenge or justice even mattered to Hunter from that moment on. Forgiveness and forgetting, however, would never come. She believed in one fateful moment a crazed human being had instantly taken everything from her.

And losing him had only gotten harder. Time had not healed her, or softened the shock and the pain in her soul. She took care of herself. She continued to thrive in her career, and nurture the relationships that meant the most to her. But finding love again would never be an option. Hunter was certain of that.

She turned over and closed her eyes on the tear-stained pillow. She was most vulnerable when there was no one else around. And the cameras were off.

Chapter 3

Sebastian Perry periodically scanned the feed from the cameras throughout the rest of the night. He felt as if he was checking them a little too diligently. If anything were amiss in Hunter Raine's massive estate, he would be alerted. There was absolutely no need to stare at the screens every five minutes. But yet he did, because there was something about her. He knew her story, so the evident pain in her eyes was understood when he scanned the camera close to her face as she spoke to him in her kitchen. She was a woman lost, and still reeling from heartache. Sebastian could relate.

He had not seen her on camera since she left the kitchen at twenty-three minutes after two in the morning. He had watched her rid the floor of broken glass. After she toweled away the spilled water, she used a cordless vacuum that she retrieved from the pantry. Sebastian was oddly impressed. There was no staff who arrived at the break of dawn for that sort of thing. Hunter took care of the unexpected mess herself in the wee hours of the morning.

He felt uncomfortable watching her at first. As if he was some sort of creeper. Her body was fit. Her arms and legs had some definition evident in the muscles. She was feminine and curvy. Truly a beautiful woman. And sexy as hell in her underwear. But what made her even more attractive was her self-assurance. The fact that she knew Sebastian was on the receiving end of that camera feed, watching her, because that was his job, and it hadn't bothered her in the least. Bash had never seen a woman so confident. She was entirely comfortable with her body, while wearing very little to cover up.

Long after Hunter left the kitchen to retreat to the private quarters of her house, Sebastian couldn't shake her from his mind. It had been eighteen months since he lost his wife. He never thought about, or had the slightest bit of interest in, another woman. There was something about Hunter Raine. He should keep those unexpected, nagging thoughts to himself though, as she was his boss. His transfer to her security team was going to be a good move for him financially. He knew he couldn't do anything to screw that up.

At the shift change at six o'clock in the morning, Jay Marks showed up to relieve him of his duty. "Morning, Bash." Jay, the large, broad-chested man who was the chief of this security team, sat down on the chair on wheels beside him. "Quiet night, I assume?" Jay's head was completely shaven and he had no inkling of facial hair. His appearance was clean, but tough. Sebastian was in shape, and tall, and strong, but not nearly as bulked up. He also had a full head of black hair and overnight scruff on his cheeks and chin at the moment. Okay, so that facial hair was a few days old. He liked the look.

"Not so quiet at two a.m. when Ms. Raine came down to the kitchen for a glass of water and accidently shattered it on the floor."

"Oh. The alarm alerted you, I hope. Did you call her?" Contacting her was protocol. She needed to know she was being protected. If something alerted them, they always followed up with Hunter. The idea was to make her feel safe and secure at all times.

"I did. She was more concerned about who the hell I was."

Jay Marks laughed. "She's a feisty one. I will see to it that you meet her soon. I typically inform her of any new hires, but it's been crazy on my end."

"Your wife and kids okay?" Sebastian felt a little too envious of any man who had a wife — and a family.

"They are, thank you," was all he offered in response.

Sebastian turned his head when camera one, in the kitchen, sounded from the movement in the room. It was Hunter. This time her platinum blonde hair was pulled up high on her head. She wore tight black yoga pants that left none of her curves to the imagination — not that Bash had to imagine anything after already seeing her practically naked. She also wore a black tank top, with the racerback straps of a heather grey sports bra visible underneath.

"Workout time, I guess?" Bash made an obvious observation.

"Yes, third floor. She'll take a bottle of water up with her. She does most of her exercise indoors on the equipment, treadmill running included. She insists we send no one when she chooses an occasional outdoor run, but we always put a trail on her. We keep our distance, by car, but we are there."

Bash nodded, not taking his eyes off the screen — or her. And Jay Marks noticed. The way he watched her was something more than doing a thorough job. Bash had an incredible resume. His background in both law enforcement and security was stellar. He didn't need to make any effort to impress Jay Marks. But that wasn't it. He was clearly taken by Hunter Raine. That much was obvious.

¥¥¥

Sebastian was making his way out the door. He was going home to get some sleep when he heard Jay Marks comment, "She's headed outdoors for a run," as he faced the camera screens.

"I'll go," Sebastian immediately spoke up.

"You will? You're on your way out."

"It's a matter of blocks before I can catch up to her. Just text me the streets she turns on along her route."

"Sounds good. Go. But remember to keep your distance. The lady wants protection most times, but she likes her space when she's running. Makes no sense to me, but just trail her." Bash was already out the door, and suddenly feeling far from tired.

Hunter's destination was Layfette Park. She used to run endless miles around that downtown neighborhood when she lived in the high-rise there. She missed that. She wished to have back a lot of things about her old life.

Sebastian took his time circling downtown Detroit. He had his eyes on her, from a distance at first, and then he ended up parking alongside of the road near the park where she appeared to be getting in the most of her run. He wasn't overly concerned about her seeing him. After all, they had never met.

Hunter ran past his parked car three consecutive times before she used her cell phone strapped to her shoulder to call Jay Marks.

"Yes?" he answered on the first ring.

"I'm at the park, downtown, on a run. Tell me that you defied my wishes and you have a trail on me. A dark-haired man with a high collar on his black jacket is watching me from a parked car."

"You should quit TV journalism and come work for me," Jay Marks chuckled, and Hunter instantly sighed in relief. She was still running, but she had considerably slowed her pace on the opposite side of the park to make this phone call.

"Who is he?" Hunter asked, but she already had a feeling this was the new guy behind the camera feed last night.

Bash.

How could she forget a name like that?

"Sebastian Perry. He's good, Hunter. Don't give him any grief."

"He alarmed me. If you're going to have someone follow me when I run, at least have them stay back a block or two so I can pretend they are not there."

Jay Marks shook his head. She was a piece of work. "Run up to his car. Introduce yourself. But be nice."

This time Hunter laughed. "I'm always nice."

Her intention was to do just that. To introduce herself to the newest member of her security team. She picked up her pace and circled the grounds before she was again close to passing his parked car. When she was two cars away from him, a man (young, probably very early twenties) abruptly left a nearby bench and stood directly in her path.

Sebastian was watching. He saw him all along. That was the reason he parked his car right there and waited.

Hunter was startled and her heart rate, which was already racing from the run, instantly quickened.

"Hi… Hunter Raine, right?" The young man smiled. It wasn't a silly starstruck smile though. This was, Hunter thought, weird.

"Yes. Excuse me," she spoke, in an attempt to get by him. But he didn't move from her path.

"Don't be rude," the young man with beady eyes and stringy brown hair spoke to her in an agitated tone. "I'd like an autograph."

Hunter wasn't having this, and when the young man reached inside of his jacket for what she hoped with all of her being was going to be a pen or a marker, she quickly bent her body forward for the mace she kept in the faux ankle brace on her right foot. She never had the chance to retrieve it, as her new bodyguard abruptly made his way out of his car.

"Step away from her," Sebastian spoke in a calm but forceful manner, as the young man spun around to find himself caught. He was going to reach for the Sharpie in his jacket pocket. He did want an autograph. On his skin. Not on paper. He also planned to put a little scare in her. Fear that was past due.

"No worries, sir," the young man feigned innocence. "Just looking for an autograph from our star here." He showed his Sharpie in hand. Sebastian was six-foot-four and he towered him.

"It's time for you to move on," Sebastian's tone was adamant, and Hunter never took her eyes off him. She was still feeling shaken, but incredibly relieved he was there for her.

The young man took a few steps away, but then turned back. This time he ignored Sebastian and only made eye contact with Hunter. "I'll see you again, sometime."

Hunter ignored him, and looked away, until he finally walked off.

Sebastian stepped closer, toward her.

"You're okay," he reassured her, and she found it interesting that he told her she was *okay* and had not asked her otherwise. She only nodded in response. "I'm Bash, from last night," was all he said to her to clarify.

"Yes, I know," she responded. "I saw you watching me, so I verified you with Jay Marks."

"Observant and smart," he complimented her, but she chided herself for not noticing the real stranger in the park. She didn't live in fear though. She had serious security in her home, but she didn't want to live her entire life sheltered or guarded.

Sebastian's cell phone rang, and she watched him answer it. He had dark eyes, dark hair, and a chiseled jawline. He expected this call as he had requested backup, with the intent to have Hunter's *fan* followed once he chased him away. Sebastian would stay with Hunter. Someone had to protect her. And he was taken aback by how much he wanted to.

"What do you have for me?" he said, into the phone, and paused to listen. "Nice work. And thanks for your help." Sebastian ended the call and faced Hunter. "Let me drive you back home."

She would agree, because she was too shaken to run, but he didn't need to know that. "First, tell me who he was. Your guy just now had some information. Share it, or you can keep your offer to give me a lift home."

Sebastian smirked. "Let's go. This isn't the place to hang around right now. You'll get your information, just not here." Hunter reluctantly obliged and followed him to his vehicle.

The moment she closed the passenger door, she noticed the scent of after shave or cologne. Clean. Fresh. But manly. His hands on the steering wheel were large. Well manicured, but strong. He could have effortlessly manhandled the scrawny guy in the park. Hunter forced her eyes forward. Before he shifted the car into reverse, she spoke to him.

"I know you're hiding something. Who was he?"

Sebastian turned to her. There was something about her, and he immediately recognized how intimate it felt to be that close to her inside the car. Her face was makeup-free and flushed from exercise. Her white blonde hair, pulled back, was matted on her forehead and curling by her ears. And there were sweat beads on her neck, and lower. That tank top, layered with a sports bra underneath, concealed very little.

"Jimmy Jenkins." Sebastian waited for her response.

All of the air felt as if it had been sucked out of her lungs. He had the same beady eyes. It was as if she knew the moment she saw him back there, face to face with her, in the park, and blocking her path. She didn't fear strangers. But she had detected danger before in her life. Those incidents just a few years ago when Ricky Jenkins was stalking her were again front and center in her mind. He wasn't harmless then either, and now that exact belief and uneasy feeling had resurfaced. The pit of her stomach hurt.

Hunter regained enough composure to speak. "Do you know what happened three years ago?" Before he could respond, because yes he knew, Hunter continued talking, and Sebastian allowed her to. "I was being stalked by a crazed fucker. He took my fiancé's life. This isn't coincidental, is it, Bash?" The way she said his name made him feel things he had not in such a long time. His entire being responded to this woman. "Ricky and Jimmy Jenkins are related, aren't they?'

"He's his little brother. He's 19 now." Hunter felt bile rise in her throat. *He was just a kid then. So impressionable. What in the world had he learned from his older brother?*

"Don't tell me he's harmless. I already fear what this means. Is this kid out for some sort of justice or revenge against me?" Hunter had taken extreme measures to feel safe after her fiancé was so ruthlessly taken from her. And suddenly, knowing there was another one out there, she felt helpless.

"I won't pass this off as nothing just to ease your mind," Sebastian began. "You're a big girl. You can handle yourself — and at the very same time, your team is going to protect you." Hunter wanted to ask him to take her to Jay Marks. She felt safest with him. He always had a plan. But she never spoke that request. Because there was also something comforting about this person who she was sharing space with right now inside that black sedan with charcoal gray leather interior. He was a brand-new addition to her team. And she already felt safe with him.

"He's free though," she stated as a matter of fact. "Just like his brother was all those times he sent threatening fan mail, or followed me in public, and eventually approached me and got too close, brushed my shoulder with his, or touched my hand. There was nothing law enforcement could do. A restraining order didn't stop him from literally showing up on my doorstep to take away the one thing I wanted most in my life." She caught her breath for a moment. "And now his brother showed up, and he too is shady and scary, and also roaming free."

"He is," Sebastian confirmed, "but he has a record. Theft. Drugs. An assault accusation, with no formal charges." Hunter momentarily closed her eyes. "He's being watched, especially after today. They'll get him. It's only a matter of time."

"I want to go home," she spoke adamantly. "I need to get showered and make it to the studio for my late-morning segment."

"Of course," Sebastian responded. She wanted to focus on work. There was a guarded wall around her again. Momentarily, he saw her vulnerability. He respected her coping mechanism though. But the kind of pain she carried had a way of slowly chipping away at a soul. He understood all too well.

Chapter 4

Hunter plopped down in the hair chair. She partially covered her bare legs with the bottom of her seafoam green robe. Aggie was ready for her, as the rush to prep everyone for the early morning newscast had passed. Hunter's segment was airing at ten a.m. today.

"You made it here safely," Aggie spoke, sounding relieved. She knew what happened. Of course she knew. Her husband was utilizing years of training and expertise in the military and in law enforcement to keep her best friend safe.

Hunter looked at her through the mirror. "One of the perks of having a driver and security, all in one," she quipped. She was making light of something serious, even though Aggie could see past the façade.

"Jay isn't messing around with this," Aggie stated, in reference to her husband's position as chief of the security team whose only mission was to keep Hunter Raine safe. "And you shouldn't either."

"What am I supposed to do? Stay tucked inside my house? I'm not going to stop living, and I'm certainly not going to exist in fear." She lied. She was feeling afraid again. She didn't want to retreat back to the time in her life when she had to look over her shoulder everywhere she went. Or be on guard when anyone approached her. She was in the public eye. She had thousands of viewers who were fond of her. And she enjoyed the attention. Most of the time. Not everyone was a nutcase.

"This time you have protection, and you need to take advantage of that. It's okay to rely on them. Jay told me that Sebastian Perry rescued you at the park today."

"I guess it was sort of a rescue," Hunter admitted. "I don't know what would have happened if I was alone. I do appreciate having security," she added in reference to Aggie's advice to utilize those men to keep her safe. She wasn't unappreciative, even though sometimes she felt as if she had very little privacy.

Aggie swept up the hair on Hunter's head with her fingers. Today she would style an updo. She knew she enjoyed them, and this morning they had the extra time. "My mother-in-law is going to watch the kids for a few days this week if you want to have a sleepover. I'll bring wine." It was a rarity for Aggie to be away from her boys, four and six years old, so Hunter immediately wanted to question her motive.

"Jay isn't going to like that," Hunter partly teased. "With the kids away, aren't parents supposed to play? You don't want to waste that potential time for passion on getting into PJs with me."

Aggie rolled her eyes and forced a laugh. "Jay Marks is hardly deprived," she giggled, and then ultimately she lost her footing behind Hunter's chair. She gripped the back of the chair to catch herself with one hand, and then she quickly let go of Hunter's hair in her other hand, to refrain from pulling it.

"You okay, there?" Hunter was taken by surprise. There was nothing to trip over, behind that chair, or so she thought.

"Yeah, um, my ankle just gave out, that's all. It happens sometimes." Aggie looked uncomfortable as she spoke. Their friendship was way past ever being uneasy or embarrassed about anything, which puzzled Hunter for a moment.

Aggie started again on styling Hunter's updo, until her hand twitched and she backed away, leaving Hunter's long blonde locks in disarray. Some of it was half up and held with bobby pins and the rest was down and on her shoulders. "Let's just keep it down today, okay?" Aggie spoke, and her facial expression was forlorn.

"Sure," Hunter agreed, but then she spun her chair around to face her. "What's going on? If you're worried about me, I am going to be just fine. You said so yourself, I have a top-notch security team protecting me."

"It's been happening too frequently," Aggie spoke, and her voice cracked. Initially, Hunter thought she wasn't making any sense. "I lose my balance because my ankle or knee will give out. I slurred my words the other day on the phone with the school secretary. My hands feel weak sometimes when I'm doing hair." Panic rose in Hunter's chest. The two of them knew everything about each other. Their secrets, their dreams, their desires. Their likes and dislikes. The names of the first boys they kissed. Who they lost their virginity to. Their family history.

Hunter thought of Aggie's grandmother, who died at sixty-nine years old of Amyotrophic Lateral Sclerosis. ALS was a disease that killed nerve cells, disabling a person, and ultimately it's fatal. What Hunter remembered about the disease that plagued Aggie's once plump and vibrant grandmother was that at the end of her life she was wheelchair bound and speechless. That awful disease had robbed her of her mobility and communication, and so much more.

Hunter abruptly stood up. Her seafoam green robe slightly gaped open at the top. One of her bare breasts was partially exposed. She didn't move to cover herself. She stared at Aggie long and hard. She wanted to speak, but she felt frozen. And terrified of the truth. Eventually, it was Aggie who spoke.

"If someone were to walk in here right now and see you with your boob hanging out, they would assume we are carrying on, and they'd sell our sultry story to the tabloids…" It was easier to make jokes right now.

"Oh for fuck's sake. People know me around here, and most have seen me flash a tit or two."

Aggie laughed out loud, but Hunter remained serious. Her face was stone cold. And when Aggie spoke the truth, Hunter wanted to cover her ears and simultaneously scream at the very top of her lungs to prevent herself from hearing any and all of it. "Only five to ten percent of people can inherit ALS," she began. "I was so certain that I was in the ninety-to-ninety-five percent that would escape it." A tear rolled from underneath Aggie's dark wire-rimmed glasses and down her cheek as she spoke. Her matching dark hair was pulled back into a low ponytail. Near her ears, Hunter for the first time could see a few lighter hairs. At any other given time, that would have been catastrophic for either of them. Typically, these women in their thirties would have damned the way gray hair gradually seeped in to steal their youth. But, now, something much more shattering was going to creep into her life. Into *both* of their lives.

"No…" Hunter whimpered, as she reached for Aggie's hands and held them, gripped them intensely, with her own. "You caught it early, right? There has to be some benefit to that, isn't there? Ags, come on, you're the strongest woman I know. You can overcome this!"

"Correction," Aggie said, holding hands with Hunter still, and stepping further into her personal space. There were no boundaries between the closest of friends. "*You* are the strongest. I'm going to need some of that courage and bravery, you hear?" Hunter released her hands from hers and pulled her in. As near as the two of them could get. Directly in her ear, she heard Aggie take a stabilizing deep breath through her nostrils, and then she completely let go of the effort she was making to be strong and fearless, and finally she just sobbed into Hunter's long blonde hair.

¥¥¥

Hunter was back home that evening. By herself. She sat in her massive living room on one of the ivory-colored sofas. She had stripped down to a black spaghetti-strapped cami with loose, baggy white sweatpants from Victoria's Secret PINK collection. Her feet were bare and curled up underneath her bottom. She held her third glass of wine in her hand. She was at the bottom of the bottle tonight.

All her life, Hunter upheld the greater need in practically every relationship. Her love for journalism began with a natural-born talent she believed in. And when she flourished in front of the camera, she only craved more of the spotlight. She needed to be on that television screen more than anyone else needed to watch her. Sure, she had fans and followers. But, in turn, Hunter desired the viewership and the ratings more than the people had to be informed or entertained. Her need was greater.

And then there was Aaron Cooper. *Cooper.* The cameraman who stole her heart. Hunter had fallen hard for him, and he for her. One of the things she immediately loved about him was the pride and confidence he carried, and how she could completely trust him to never take advantage of her fame or fortune. She used to tell him that he knew the real her, because she had been able to give him all of her being. He completed her, and without him Hunter swore she would no longer feel whole. Her great love would laugh and dub her as silly and he never missed a chance to remind her that a woman like her could stand on her own. Cooper told her he was the lucky one to be by her side. And to have her heart. Even still, Hunter believed her need for him was greater.

Aggie was the one constant in Hunter's circle. The one who never left. Always there. She knew Hunter the best of anyone. They were in each other's lives before they were women, when they were just preteens and later teenage girls trying to sift through the confusing thoughts and feelings and changes with their bodies. Hunter took a long sip of the white wine in her glass. She may have succeeded at acting like the strong one. Perhaps she wanted Aggie to perceive her as such. But, really, Hunter always needed her best girlfriend a little more than Aggie ever needed her back. And here she was again. Feeling lost and alone. And she was alone. And one day, probably sooner than she wanted to admit, her best friend would not be standing behind the hair chair… or just a phone call or a car ride away.

The wine glass in her hand was empty, and she had half a mind to throw it as hard as she could at that floor or against the nearest wall. *Life sucked. The unexpected pain that had been hurled at her was just too much to accept this time.*

So now what?

There was another bottle of wine in the refrigerator.

But first, there was a soft knock at the main front door to her house.

Chapter 5

The interior camera monitor revealed who waited on the opposite side of the door on her massive front porch with white Corinthian columns. Hunter had not been alerted that someone punched in the code to enter through the estate's gate, because her cell phone had been powered off. She turned the deadbolt and opened the door.

"Bash? Why are you here?"

He watched her segment on ABS NewsChannel 7 today. He had seen Hunter Raine's face on television before, maybe heard her in the background from the same or another room in his house, but today was different. He really watched. Focused on her. And listened. She was unbelievably talented. She was also incredibly beautiful. The pain in her eyes was gone when she was in front of the camera. She was a born actress. A true star on the television screen.

But then he watched her come home. On the real-life camera feed, she was withdrawn. Sad. Forlorn. Lonely. And consuming a lot of alcohol. When Sebastian inquired about this sudden change in her, Jay Marks confided in him. He told him what happened. He revealed the sad, incredibly unfortunate, and impossible-to-grasp truth of Aggie's fate.

And that's when Sebastian decided to reach out. To take a chance. He felt compelled to. He wanted to. But he was forewarned. *Hunter Raine doesn't let anyone in too easily anymore. Especially not anyone new into her heart.*

"I could say I'm making a house call for camera number two on the third floor. It's acting up. Feeding in and out, regularly. But," he admitted, "I'm actually here to check on you. I know about your best friend... Jay's wife."

Hunter stood in place, still in the doorway inside her home, and Sebastian remained on the porch. This wasn't the norm for her. No one outside of her circle typically checked on her, not unless they wanted something from her. "And I assume you saw me on camera looking like quite the lush tonight," she spoke sarcastically. It was just easier to be snarky, than to let herself feel any more pain.

That too, he wanted to say, but refrained, because everyone needed an outlet sometimes. But he only smiled at her. His dark eyes. Dark hair. He was so dang tall. Broad-shouldered. Massive hands. Yet he was a gentle man. At least that's what Hunter had assumed thus far. She really didn't know him that well.

They shared silence for a moment. Hunter watched him put his hands in the front pockets of his dark-washed denim, and rock back and forth on his heels. He obviously wasn't going anywhere. He couldn't be chased away that easily.

"So, are you going to come in and repair that camera or not?" she asked, and he chuckled at the sudden silly grin on her face. It was the most real he had seen her be, perhaps yet.

Sebastian stepped inside and waited while Hunter closed the door and turned the deadbolt. She saw him watching her. "It's what I do," she felt the need to explain.

"I understand," he said, but really he didn't. The property and the land she had out there deserved to be enjoyed. *Open the windows, sit out on the porch. Savor it. Relish it. Live like no one was watching.* But he suspected she never did any of that, and she sadly had a justifiable reason not to. He wondered if she truly lived in a state of constant fear. She didn't appear to.

"Then what are you thinking?" she called him out, as she moved away from the front door, and stopped again a few feet from him. He wore a fitted black t-shirt with tapered denim and brown tie boots that covered his ankles. She didn't have shoes on to give her any height at all, so he seemed even more like a giant beside her five-foot-five frame.

"That I hope you do not live in fear," he said, honestly.

"I really don't," she was quick to answer. "I just know the smart things I need to do to protect myself. That mindset became a habit for me after Coop was—" Hunter paused, "killed."

"I want you to know that you can trust me the same as Jay Marks and everyone else on your security team. I will keep you safe. The incident in the park has you rattled again. But I want you to have peace of mind knowing that Jenkins number two is on our watch list."

Hunter listened, and she felt sickened at the thought of there even being another monster like the one who ruined her life. "Can I share something with you?" she asked, and he nodded. His eyes moved over that black camisole and white sweatpants. It wasn't a typical look, nor was it even trendy, but she was confident and sexy in it. Sebastian was attracted to her. Not just her body though. He felt intoxicated just listening to her speak. She was strong and smart, and there was an eloquence about her that was extremely captivating. "When you have someone in your world that completes you… and that person is suddenly snatched away and never coming back… it changes you." Sebastian understood that more than Hunter realized, and he wanted to share his story with her, too, eventually. "It hardens you. It almost takes some of the fear out. I don't think I'm making any sense." Hunter abruptly stopped talking, as she walked over to the sofa table where she left her empty wine glass. She wanted to ask him if he would like a drink, just so she could get herself more. Sebastian followed her. He watched her eye that empty glass.

"It's harsh," she spoke again, "but true. I really don't care what happens to me anymore." *And now,* she thought, *her best friend was gradually going to slip away from herself, her family, and this life. And Hunter.*

Sebastian was quiet. She didn't even want to look at him after she spoke something so raw from her soul. "It's all too much sometimes," he finally said. "Hardships can destroy us. But, if you can't find the will to carry on for yourself, then do it for someone else."

"Like my best friend who's now dying?" she spoke bitterly.

"She's going to need you."

"Yes, I know. And then, when she leaves me too — I'll be alone to scrape what's left of me off the ground again. Well fuck that. I just don't have it in me anymore." She shook her head at the thought of it all. "You can show yourself upstairs for that camera issue. I need something to drink." She gave up on talking. And she walked away from him. He watched her. She made it practically all the way out of the room to where she was going to turn the corner to enter the kitchen, and he raised his voice to catch her attention.

"You're talking to someone who understands more than you know. I get it." Hunter looked back at him. There was so much space between them now. Distance. She realized as she walked away from him that she was beginning to feel too comfortable. And her only reaction was to flee.

"Thanks," was all she replied. "I pretty much told you that I don't care if the next crazy fan takes me out, and you nod along and tell me you get it. Nice. So do you want to go drown ourselves in the pool out back? If you get it, as you claim, you would completely understand that life has forced me to lose my will to live."

"I don't want to end my life, nor do you want to either," he spoke for her, and she was unnerved. "I've been on the edge before, I think we all have — but there's a difference between feeling fed up, and seriously giving up."

"I'm not suicidal, so don't spread that bullshit around. I've just surrendered to fate. Come and get me."

Sebastian walked the entire length of the room to get to her. His legs were long, and his stride was relaxed and confident. Hunter never moved. She just watched him, and her heartbeat quickened. He needed to leave. She wanted to ask him to.

He stopped very close to her, and he stared down at her until she felt compelled to look up at him. "There. Now you see that I am here," he was referring to her finally looking at him. "I know you wish I would just walk away, bolt through that door and resume my position on your security team and that is all. You don't want to let anyone in. It's too risky to think you could lose someone again."

"You don't know me," she lied, as she tried to hide the fact that she truly was taken aback by his ability to read her so well.

"No, not too well," he replied, "but well enough."

"To what?" she demanded. "Take me to bed? Is that what you're after? I'm not afraid to take my clothes off for sex. But I don't fall in love and I don't make love anymore. I don't commit long enough to anyone for that."

Sebastian tried to hide his attraction for her. What he really wanted to do was force her into his arms and kiss her until she gave in to what he already believed was something incredible between them. *Attraction. Combustion. Passion.* "And I don't take advantage of a woman who has been drinking."

"You think I'm drunk?" she resented his words. "I'm not, but what would it matter if I was? I just found out that my best friend is going to die. But not before she suffers. Not before she has to tear herself away from her children and her husband. How fucking unfair!" Hunter choked up, but quickly composed herself. She did not allow herself to fall apart in front of anyone. Least of all, strangers.

"I'm sorry," he told her, sincerely, and again he resisted the urge to physically comfort her.

"Just go. Send someone else for the camera. I want to be alone."

She was, after all, his boss. She gave him an order. Sebastian knew he needed to respect her wishes to leave her home. He very quickly began to care about her, and Sebastian wanted to defy her request right now, and try harder to reach her. To hell with repairing the camera upstairs. He wanted to talk to her more. Maybe hold her hand. Or pull her into his arms and embrace her body with his own. To comfort her. To seriously surrender to the temptation to discover how it would feel to be close to her.

He didn't say anything. He just turned away from her, and made his way to the front door. He unlocked the deadbolt before he looked back at her. She was still standing where he left her. A part of him believed she would have escaped to the kitchen by now. *To get a drink. Or, just run from him.*

"I didn't come here to have sex with you," he began, and he had her attention. "The last woman I made love to was my wife." Hunter felt her eyes widen. *He was married.* She had never noticed that he wore a wedding ring. "That was eighteen months ago, before she died tragically in a car accident that stole all of the hopes and dreams that I had left in this life. So when I say that I get it, I understand precisely what you're feeling. I get those dark, hopeless thoughts. I damn well do."

He opened the door now and closed it swiftly behind him. At the very same time, Hunter had raised her hand to her mouth in sheer surprise, but she spoke too late, "Bash..." just as the door shut and he was gone.

Chapter 6

Sebastian drove to downtown Detroit after he left Hunter's estate in the suburbs. She had pissed him off. Or maybe he was more upset with himself for falling for her. She told him so herself, she didn't let anyone into her heart. Even still, Sebastian imagined himself being able to reach her. And maybe to heal her somehow. By loving her. *God, he had it bad.*

He parked his car and entered the lobby of a building that housed a coffee shop and a local newspaper dubbed, The Detroit Journal. In that lobby, he took the elevator downstairs to the rented space and private quarters where Hunter's security team operated. The cameras were always live, and their destination was less than ten miles from Hunter's estate, for the purpose of being close by if she physically needed help.

He stepped off the elevator in the basement and almost bumped directly into Jay Marks. "Whoa, you headed out?" Sebastian asked him.

"I'm going home. I need to be there for Ags. She put the kids to bed and she's alone and thinking too much."

"Say no more," Sebastian said, holding up his hand between them. What he wouldn't give to be with his wife one last time. "Go. I've got this covered tonight."

"Good. I was going to text you on my way out. It should be quiet," Jay Marks referred to the cameras. "Only thing is, Jackson has the night off, so if Hunter decides she needs a driver, you'll have to go."

Sebastian doubted Hunter would leave her home tonight. She was likely drowning her sorrows in more wine by now. But he did ask, "What about manning the camera feed?"

"Leave it," Jay Marks said. "As long as you are with her, she's safe. And that's our objective."

¥¥¥

Just minutes later, he looked twice at the caller identification when his cell phone rang. It was Jay Marks. He couldn't have been any farther than the parking lot.

"Yeah?" Sebastian answered the call.

"She wants to go out. I told her I'd send a driver. She thinks it's going to be her usual escort. Surprise her."

"Oh shit," was Sebastian's response, and Jay Marks chuckled as he ended the call.

¥¥¥

Sebastian again punched in the security code at the gate of the estate and then drove his black sedan into the circle drive. The front door of the house opened the moment he shifted his car into park. Even in the dark, she knew it was him. He watched her make her way down the wide, well-lit steps of the wrap-around porch. She was still wearing that black camisole, now with an off-the-shoulder ivory sweater overtop. And she had changed into a tight pair of dark-washed denim with black heels. She walked confidently in high heels. Sebastian didn't know what distracted him more right now — those heels, or the fact that she was still not wearing a bra underneath that lacy, loose-fitting little thing. He forced those thoughts from his mind the moment she opened the back door of his car.

"Seriously?" she peeked only her head inside first. "Where's Jackson? He's my driver."

"Not working tonight. It's me or no one. Get in, but not the backseat. The front, please."

Hunter rolled her eyes and slammed the back door shut. Sebastian chuckled under his breath because she had actually listened to him. She plopped down onto the seat, poked her heels on the floormat, and then shut her door. She stayed silent as she buckled her seatbelt around her upper body. She smelled good. As if she just spritzed perfume all over herself.

"So, are you going to tell me where we're going at almost ten o'clock at night? When I left, you were practically in your jammies and had enough alcohol to send you to bed for the night."

"Don't be an ass," she began, "and, *we* are not going anywhere. You can drop me off at Standby." Sebastian was well aware of that innovative bar on Gratiot Avenue. He was the only security she had tonight. *Like hell if he would just wait in the car.* He failed to ask Jay Marks if anyone was tailing Jenkins tonight. That was reason enough for him not to let Hunter out of his reach. And besides, he could use a drink.

"Not happening. I have orders. I'll be going in for a beer."

That, she'll have to see, Hunter thought, *because he needed to loosen up.*

¥¥¥

She wasn't at all used to walking in anywhere with a man at her side. Not since Cooper. Sure, her security guys sometimes served as escorts or bodyguards, however she preferred to see it, but this time was different. Sebastian, still wearing his tight black t-shirt with tapered denim and those tie work boots, towered her —even in her high heels— and she liked how it felt to have him beside her, like some sort of protective shield. She wasn't ready to admit to herself that she felt anything more.

Hunter caught the bartender's (and everyone else's) eye the moment she walked in. Most people were courteous and respectful of her privacy and left her alone. She was hardly a hermit and the public was accustomed to seeing her out and about, almost as much as she was on their televisions. Sebastian allowed her to take the lead, as he was only supposed to be along for the ride. And to make sure no one impeded her space, or safety. She went directly up to the bar.

"We're grabbing a booth tonight," she told the young bartender. "Two longnecks when you're ready, Dominic."

When the bartender returned, Sebastian placed a wad of cash on the bar and grabbed both bottles. "After you," he said to Hunter and she crisscrossed her handbag on her body and gave him a lopsided grin. *She wasn't the only one who could be full of surprises.*

They slipped into the booth on opposite sides. Hunter twisted off the bottle cap and took the first sip. Sebastian watched her. "You didn't strike me as the beer-drinking type."

"Oh I'm not," she immediately responded. "I'll have one, and then I'll feel all bloated and burpy, so I'll get a glass of wine."

Sebastian chuckled, and shook his head for a moment.

"What?" she pressed him.

"Why are you here? Don't you have an early newscast in the morning for which you'll need to be bright-eyed?" Given the fact that she had been drinking tonight, Sebastian was surprised her eyes were clear and she acted and appeared to be completely sober.

"I am around people all day long. My makeup is done for me, my hair," she paused, thinking of Aggie, and the dreadful idea of someone else filling her spot behind that hair chair. "Everything is handled for me. And then I'm on camera, performing for thousands of viewers. My days are long and full of constant chatter and directions and opinions and feedback. And then I go home, and it's complete silence. I can't stand it sometimes. I have to get out, and hear the ruckus of the world around me just to keep myself sane."

She needed someone in her life. A man by her side again, Sebastian thought. *A husband and a couple of kids, eventually.* It was human nature. He took a long swig of his beer and spoke what was going through his mind. "You're lonely. I'm not sure bar-hopping is the answer for that though."

"I like the scene here. My friend, Christian owns this place. I don't see him around tonight though. He's not always here. He's the business man behind it, but he prefers to have other people run things for him."

"It's a laidback atmosphere, much like a lounge," Sebastian commented. "How's the food here?"

"Delicious," Hunter replied. "Are you hungry?"

"Yeah, I haven't had dinner yet. Been busy working," he smirked a little, and she thought of how he had been at her house earlier to fix a malfunctioning camera but he had never gotten to it as she asked him to leave. And then he was back at her place, acting as her driver and escort tonight. It suddenly occurred to her that she was being selfish.

"Be right back," she slid out of her side of the booth, and Sebastian's eyes moved to the cleavage that peeked out of the scoop neckline of her sweater as she shifted her body sideways. "I'm going to order us a few appetizers to go with these beers." He watched her in her heels, maneuver through the crowd. *She was safe. Keep her safe, Bash. Stop losing your focus on how her ass looks in those tight jeans.*

She returned to the table just a few short minutes later with a waiter following her. *When you're Detroit's leading newswoman, there was no wait for your request.* On the waiter's tray were hot wings, fried mushrooms, spinach gringo with homemade tortillas, and Sebastian stopped looking at what all else. He smiled at her across from him once the waiter left. "This looks great. Thank you."

"Anytime," she said, as she stuffed a mushroom in her mouth and made a polite attempt to close her mouth while she chewed. She meant those words. She could get used to spending time with Sebastian Perry.

¥¥¥

It was nearly midnight and a few beers later for Bash while true-to-her-word Hunter had switched back to drinking wine.

"I need five hours of sleep," she said out of the blue.

"Okay, we can get going. You're calling the shots," he told her, relieved knowing she was going to stop drinking, but selfishly he did not want to see this night end with her.

"Shots? Yes! Let's do shots!" she started to flag the bartender from their booth tucked way over into the corner, and Bash quickly grabbed her forearm and put it down. "Nope. You're already drunk. No more."

She pretended to pout, and he ignored her. She did willingly stand up then and was well-balanced in her high heels, walking beside him as they left the bar. Once in his car, she sat beside him with her head back on the seat.

"Let me know if you're going to chuck it all."

She laughed. "Just tired. I can handle my alcohol."

"You sure can," he told her, and drove her home in mostly silence. While she may have been tired, Bash's mind was reeling. He had not felt this wound up about a woman since he was deeply committed to one, sadly, 'til death do them part.

¥¥¥

Bash walked her inside and they stood in the foyer as they had earlier when their conversation became too much for Hunter to handle. Neither one of them had brought up anything about what was said then. But Hunter wanted to now.

"About what you told me earlier," she began, as he stood closest to the front door of her home, "I'm sorry that happened to you. Grief sucks."

"It sure does," he agreed.

"You can talk about it, if you want," Hunter told him. "About your wife, what she was like..."

"So can you," he told her. "About your fiancé, and how he obviously meant the world to you." She froze a little. That was not the game she wanted to play. She only wanted to hear his story, not share hers. Not yet. Maybe not ever.

He recognized her immediate tension. "You don't want to, do you?" He watched her shake her head. "It's fine. Maybe my story will help you to see that you're not alone and that life isn't fair for the rest of us either."

"You make me sound selfish," she interjected.

"No," he shook his head. "It's just reality. We feel alone when tragedy strikes us. And, we're both still sleeping with their ghosts."

Hunter took a step back from him. "I'm not sure I like how that sounds. I don't." He definitely caught her off guard with those words. But, as she stood there, she knew that it was true.

"I'm sorry," he stated. "It's too much to get into now anyway. It's late. I'll go."

She didn't want him to leave, but she stayed quiet, as he turned toward the door but then turned back around to her again. "Thanks for tonight. Lock this door when I leave, as I know you will, and I'll head back to the station to keep an eye on the cameras while you get your five hours of beauty sleep." He watched her smile. *God, she was beautiful.*

"Stay for awhile," she said, reaching for his hand, and he willingly took hers in his. This was the first time they really touched. His body instantly tightened. And she was taken aback by the warm, electric current shooting through her. *This was just going to be sex,* she told herself. *He will not stay until sunrise,* she reminded herself to make that clear to him if they went any farther with their goodbye in her grand foyer.

She initiated it. And he bent down to meet her lips with his. Her kiss was soaked in wine, as he could still taste the beer in his own mouth. But it wasn't the alcohol that was intoxicating him at the moment. *It was her.*

He deepened his kiss. She followed his lead. He pulled her closer, pressing those breasts peaking out of that camisole against his chest. She whispered, *the cameras,* and pulled away, inviting him to *come upstairs* with her. He followed, not touching her. Just watching her walk up all of those stairs. *Still in high heels. Still swaying her ass.*

When they reached her bedroom, he stayed close to her and she sat down on the end of that large, four-poster bed. He knelt on the floor in front of her. He was that tall, as their faces were now equally aligned. "I want to have sex with you, Bash," she spoke, and his entire body responded to her. He placed his hands on the sides of her face and pulled her into a slow, seductive kiss. It was going to be so good with her. This. Being with a woman like this had been too long for him. He made his way down her neck, to her collar bone, and then much lower with his tongue. He grazed the spillover of her full breasts with the tip of his tongue. He wanted her nipples out of that lace. She started to lift up her sweater at the waist for him, and he spoke hoarsely to her.

"I can't stay," he stated, and he felt as disappointed as he sounded.

"I know," she added. "Just be with me, but then you have to go."

Sebastian knew precisely what she meant. No man stayed the night, all night, with her. He had heard as much from the other security officers who protected this woman day and night. "I want to be with you more than anything right here and right now," he told her, and he kissed her lightly on the lips, making her instantly crave more of it, and all of him. "But not like this. Not on those terms. I'll stay when I can make love to you, and when you are ready to fall asleep in my arms all night long."

Sebastian regretfully backed away from her and rose to his feet. Hunter all but sunk down onto her bed. The disappointment crushed her. "You're turning me down?"

"No. I'm looking forward to something better between us." And he turned and left her bedroom without looking back.

Chapter 7

Aggie stood at the hair station that was her makeshift salon at NewsChannel 7. The curling rod and the straightener were both warm. She caught a glimpse of herself in the mirror. She inched closer and pulled at the tiny graying hairs around both of her ears, but more so the right one. She needed to conceal those. She wanted to look youthful and to feel healthy for as long as she possibly could. Today was a good day. She felt strong, and she did not have a single symptom or setback since getting out of bed this morning. Her husband had noticed, and before the kids were awake, he caught her coming out of the shower. He touched her first, and then asked her if it was okay. They ended up making love on the bathroom floor. Aggie smiled at the thought of the two of them giving in to lust and passion, like when they first met. Life just gets in the way of savoring the moment after awhile, she thought, and sometimes it unfortunately took sickness or tragedy or growing apart or anything unexpected to make people see the importance of living in the moment. Of appreciating time.

Aggie pushed her dark-rimmed glasses up on her nose. She thought of one day, who knew how soon, when she would kiss Jay for the last time. And feel the warmth of her hand in his. He was the love of her life. She would be lost without him, she always believed. But Jay, he would eventually be okay. He would continue to be a wonderful father, and of course throw himself deeper into his work. He thrived on protecting people from harm. And, someday, Aggie wished for him to find love again. She teared up at the thought of another woman in his arms. In their bed. Aggie shouldn't have to give him up. *Damn it. He was her husband.* They were supposed to be together for life. Their children were the best parts of both of them. Those boys were going to grow up to be as strong as their father and as sensitive as their mother. They would both make caring and supportive husbands one day. Having to leave her sons behind would surely kill her before that awful disease. A tear escaped and rolled down her cheek. She brushed it away before anyone walked in and saw her slowly coming apart at the seams.

Her husband and children would be okay, she told herself again. She would be in their hearts forever. The love in her life that Aggie worried most about, knowing she would no longer be here for her and able to guide her or keep her afloat at times, was Hunter. The last three years, watching her bobbing in grief, barely coming up for air, was a worry that never subsided for Aggie. *Who would be there to throw her a life preserver after I'm gone? And what if my absence completely sucks her under?* Aggie could have bawled at the mere thought, but she quickly composed herself as she was no longer alone backstage at the studio.

Hunter plopped down in the hair chair, wearing very little underneath that seafoam green robe again. "Hey honey… you were lost in thought," Hunter stated, not really needing to guess what saturated her mind.

"Just feeling very grateful for life today. *I - feel - good,"* she sang out in her best representation of the James Brown oldie. And Hunter laughed out loud.

"You suck! Stop singing!" Hunter hollered, and they both giggled in unison. Whoever overheard the two of them on mornings like this had to have been slightly jealous of their crazy connection and the silly fun they always had together.

"I'm happy you're feeling *so good,"* Hunter emphasized, smiling, as Aggie combed through her long platinum hair.

"Sex on the bathroom floor before the kids were up," Aggie winked.

Hunter let out a loud cackle before she rolled her eyes. "At least someone is getting it."

"What? Where did that come from? Your go-to Christian wasn't available for a booty call?"

"Not him. Bash was my driver last night. We talked, and drank, quite a bit at Standby. We also kissed when he brought me home. I wanted to take it further. He didn't. End of story."

"This is the new security guy? I need to know more. I've barely asked Jay or you anything about him. What in the world? Is he gay?"

"Hardly," Hunter objected. "You should see him!"

"Well I want to!" Aggie all but pouted.

"He says he cares about me, and that he understands me," Hunter paused before she clarified that Bash's words were not just come-on lines. "His wife was killed in a car accident eighteen months ago."

Aggie's eyes widened. "How terrible." She kept quiet her thoughts of how remarkably life worked. The stars were aligned after all. The timing just had to be right.

Hunter nodded in agreement. "We had a good time last night. I'm attracted to him. I told him that I wanted to have sex with him after we got close as we were saying goodbye in my foyer. I made it clear that he couldn't stay though."

"Right… no naked men in your bed all night long. Fun's over before sunrise." Aggie mocked her.

"Shut it," Hunter scolded her.

"So, let me get this straight. An attractive—"

"Actually, incredibly sexy," Hunter interjected with what she believed was a more fitting adjective.

"Okay, an incredibly sexy man turned you down? Did he give a good reason?"

"He said," Hunter paused. She already knew the response that she was going to get from Aggie. From any woman in her right mind. It was Hunter who was completely out of hers. "He said," she repeated, "that he wouldn't sleep with me on those terms. And that he will stay when he can make love to me, and when I am ready to fall asleep in his arms all night long."

"Oh. My. God. You are out of your mind!" Aggie spoke too loud backstage, and her voice likely carried to the cameramen gearing up for the early newscast on the main floor. "You are completely insane," she again reworded her opinion. This time she lowered her voice. "Most men think with the skin between their legs. Most men would have jumped you and left you lay. Who gives a hoot about the sunrise. You, honey, are letting the real thing slip right through your grasp. I can't even style your hair this morning without the urge to smack you upside the head!"

Hunter smirked a little. "Fuck you, Ags."

"No thanks," Aggie quipped.

"Great, now no one wants to!" Hunter seriously whined, before they both succumbed to laughter.

And when the giggling subsided, Aggie spun the hair chair around and bent forward to look her best friend directly in the eyes. They were so close that Aggie could smell the spearmint gum that Hunter was chewing to cover up the lingering taste of last night's alcohol. "Don't be stupid."

"I'm not!" Hunter insisted.

"No?" Aggie's tone begged to differ, and Hunter spun her chair back around.

"No," Hunter stated as a matter of fact. "I'm afraid."

Aggie softened. She wrapped her arms around the back of Hunter's chair and clasped her hands across the front of her chest.

"What is this, a chair hug?" Hunter tried to lighten everything between them.

"Sure, and when are you going to start wearing a bra?" Aggie moved her hands off of Hunter's bare chest beneath her robe. They both grinned and suppressed giggles. The jokes always came when things got too serious between them.

"Aggie?" Hunter caught her eyes in the mirror before she finally started to get to work on her hairstyle for morning TV. "Thanks for loving me… despite how difficult I am to understand."

Aggie could have cried, but she didn't. This practically lifelong girlfriend of hers needed her. And for as long as she could be, Aggie was going to be there for her. "No thanks necessary. And I get you, I really do. It's you who misunderstands yourself, if that's even possible."

Hunter stayed silent.

"You've forgotten how to be happy. You are so swallowed up, almost to the point of being oddly comfortable, in your own pain. Yes, you were dealt an unfair and tragic loss that will hurt you forever. But no one expects you to stay there."

"What suddenly makes you Dear Abby? Where has this advice been for me for the last few years?" Hunter wanted to know, because it actually made sense. And Aggie had never confronted her like this before. *Was it because she was now given notice that her own life was going to be cut unfairly short?* This time, Hunter could have cried.

"There's never been a Bash before," was all Aggie said.

"You haven't even met him," Hunter argued with a solid fact.

"I don't need to. I see the way you look when you speak of him," Aggie sighed and smiled.

"I don't want anything to happen again. To him. Or, to my heart." This was a huge admission for Hunter to make to herself, and especially aloud.

"Hunter. Please listen to me. And listen well. Happiness is a right. We are all entitled to it. Seize it while you can, for God's sake. Choose it when it's at your fingertips, or stretch to reach it if it's not. Before it's too late."

Chapter 8

Her hair looked sleek, brushed straight back, and tied and twisted into a neat bun just above the nape of her neck. The style revealed more of her dark roots underneath that platinum blonde coating. It was a simple and easy hairdo today, given the fact that Hunter and Aggie had taken up most of the prep-time talking. As Aggie watched her now from the backstage monitor, live on air, she wondered if she had really gotten through to her. It was difficult to tell if anything would change, because Hunter fiercely protected her own heart.

"If I had the opportunity to rewind time, to go back to my teenage years when I was in high school, and do it all over again, I wouldn't," Hunter spoke directly into the camera as she began her segment. "Why? Because I was bullied. I believed my nose was too long for my face. I struggled with periodic acne. I had no confidence in myself at all. Not with my appearance, nor in my ability to socialize with my peers. On the plus side, I was a very good student and I had one best friend," Hunter kept her composure as she thought of all she and Aggie had been through and how their journey as sisters-by-heart would end much sooner than either of them ever would have foreseen. She forced herself to regain complete focus as she spoke to her Detroit audience. "Thank goodness for my best girlfriend, or I may have turned to all sorts of things that kids seek when they are forsaken by their peers and made fun of at such a delicate, awkward stage of life. Bullying is a real problem that's on the rise, and it's repercussions have been devastating for so many lives when young people have chosen suicide as their only option, the only way out." Hunter paused as the camera panned wide to her guests today, seated on the two armchairs adjacent to her own.

"Jodie and Katie are here today to share their story. We are refraining from giving their last names, but we are talking in detail about their experience at Detroit Community High School. The two of you have been friends since kindergarten," both girls nodded their heads, as Hunter continued their story, "and your friendship triangle, if you will, was completed by a third member. A boy. Your friend, Sammy." Hunter watched the girls grasp hands. It was difficult already to hear the name of their good friend gone too soon. "Sammy was bullied," Hunter told the television audience, "and even the bond he shared with his close friends here could not save him from the distraught state of mind that led to him taking his own life just six months ago. Girls, we cannot stop the bullying, but we can attempt to lessen it by telling Sammy's story. Would either one of you like to share what kind of person Sammy was?"

Katie, the more outspoken of the two girls, began to speak. "Sammy was different. He walked on his tip toes, he had a lisp sometimes when he spoke too fast or if he was nervous or excited, and he struggled to get good grades. Most of the kids at school accepted him and loved him, like we did," Katie made eye contact with Jodie seated right beside her. "But then there were the bullies who judged him for being different and they wouldn't leave him alone. He was physically pushed around, and verbally harassed."

"One day, they shoved him into a trash can in the cafeteria," Jodie found her voice, to speak on behalf of the friend she lost. "We tried so hard to make him see that it would eventually pass, that they would move on to bother some other kid and finally leave him alone, but it was just too much for Sammy."

"And that's the awful part of these stories. Our young people, like Jodie and Kate here with me today, are well aware that this is an ongoing problem. When or if one bullying incident ceases, another will begin elsewhere. As Jodie now said, it's just too much. We will, however, continue to raise awareness and try to help stop this growing problem. And, in honor of National Bullying Prevention Week, I will continue this story with a segment each day. Tomorrow morning, I will be live at Detroit Community High School to kick off a special day where all of the students and staff will be asked to reach out to someone on the premises throughout the school day who they normally do not have contact with, or socialize with. The students will also have lunch with someone they never have eaten with before. I will highlight a few of those stories. Girls, I cannot thank you both enough for being here today to honor your friend, Sammy and to raise awareness to prevent bullying." The camera then panned out, just seconds before a commercial break. Today's segment was over. And Hunter took the time to hug both of the girls and to thank them *for their bravery* before she walked off the set.

Aggie was waiting for her backstage. "What the hell?" she whispered to her. "You weren't bullied, and you never had a single pimple on that long-ass nose of yours before, during, or after puberty."

"See, my nose really is too long for my face!" Hunter defended herself, as Aggie walked alongside of her to find a quieter spot backstage.

"I can't believe you lied," Aggie tried to keep her voice down.

"I didn't... I just stretched the truth a bit to help the viewers relate to me and the story on a more personal level. I meant what I said, I honestly would not want to go back to relive those days."

"You're incorrigible," Aggie shook her head. Some things would never change. Even as adults, Aggie was the straight arrow who made the right, honest choices. Hunter was the complete opposite. She lived for the moment, and acted on what felt right on an impulse.

"But you love me anyway," Hunter grinned.

¥¥¥

Bash and Jay Marks had just watched Hunter's segment on NewsChannel 7. "She's a natural," Bash commented, as Jay Marks looked at him.

"Yep. Wipe your chin, you were drooling at the screen," Jay Marks quipped, and Bash gave him the finger and then chuckled.

"She knows how I feel about her. Now I wait to see if she's as brave as she pretends to be," Bash commented.

"Oh she's brave, just not with her heart," Jay Marks spoke the truth.

"So, about that live segment tomorrow," Bash changed the subject. "Do we show up? I assume there will be a crowd of onlookers gathered on the grounds, because Hunter just publicly announced where she will be in the morning. What if Jenkins shows his face?"

"Once she and the crew are inside the school, the doors are locked and there's plenty of security. I am thinking you or I will need to be there for the outside taping as she interacts with the students upon arrival, before she goes live inside."

"I'll go," Bash volunteered.

"Of course you will," Jay Marks smirked, and then he asked, "Have you kissed her yet?"

"Yes and then I tore myself away because I'm a gentleman who's interested in sharing something more with her."

"Then you're going to be taking cold showers until the end of time," Jay Marks laughed out loud at his own comment.

"Let's hope not quite that long..." Bash dropped his elbows onto his quads and buried his face in his hands.

¥¥¥

Sebastian estimated that there were about seventy viewers or fans gathered at the high school for Hunter's live television segment on bullying. It was actually more of a crowd than he expected on a weekday morning. He had spoken to Bruce Rudis, the producer, so the on-location crew would be aware of him combing through the crowd. He, at first, tried to blend with the news crew and not quite be engulfed in the crowd of people, and that's when Hunter spotted him. She showed up looking striking in a black pencil skirt that ended just above the knees with tall black heeled boots. Her powder-blue silk blouse was unbuttoned generously, but respectably on her chest. Sebastian could see, even from a considerable distance away from her, how that color made her blue eyes pop. She was taping a thirty-second teaser for viewers that would air before she went live. She had just wrapped it up when she saw his face. She smirked a little. This was the first time they had seen each other since he left her bedroom. She didn't feel awkward or embarrassed. Disappointed, maybe, but she was a confident woman and things like that just didn't rattle her. He winked at her, and then she looked away. Hunter was working. And apparently, so was Bash. She pushed out of her head any idea that she would need security there, or that the high school campus would not be safe for the students and staff this morning.

After the third and final take outdoors, Hunter was walking alongside of her cameraman and Bruce followed them. The crowd was leaving, as the rest of the story was going to be shot inside. Sebastian breathed a little easier knowing that. There was no sign of Jenkins, but he still wanted to stay on the grounds. He texted Jay Marks as he stood outside.

I'm staying. Probably not going inside, but I'll be on the grounds.

His boss' immediate reply was, *I'm in the parking lot, keeping an eye on the news van.*

This took Sebastian by surprise, but before he had a chance to ask any questions, he looked up from his phone to find Hunter toe-to-toe with him. "Hello Bash," she said to him first.

He put his phone in the rear pocket of his denim. "Hello Hunter."

"I didn't expect for you to be here," she told him outright. "Is everything clear?" Clear was the term she heard her security team use many times before. *All was clear.*

Sebastian nodded. "Yes. Just here to keep you safe."

"Thank you. Are you going inside with us?"

"No, but I'm not leaving," he told her.

"Is there something going on that I should know about?" Hunter instantly felt uneasy.

"No, I'm sorry, I didn't mean to make you nervous."

Bruce interrupted when he called Hunter away from her conversation with Bash. Hunter glanced in his direction, and then back at Bash. He started to reach for her with his hand, but she stepped back. "Don't. No touching in public." She saw the confused look on Bash's face. "It's my way of keeping you from harm, too, okay?" her voice softened, and he instantly understood.

"What about touching in private?" he asked her, under his breath.

She suppressed a giggle, and walked away from him. Now, with a spring in her step. And a silly grin on her face.

As soon as the main front door of the school building closed behind Hunter and her team, Sebastian took his phone out of his pocket again. He immediately called Jay Marks.

He answered on the first ring. "I'm in the black pickup, one row over from the news van. Come sit in here with me." Bash ended the call without responding.

When he closed the passenger door of the pickup, Jay Marks was behind the wheel. "I had no idea you were here," Bash stated.

"Someone needed to be front and center, that was you. Someone else needed to lay low."

"Anything going on?" Bash eyed the news van.

"Jenkins never showed up in the crowd that you were monitoring — because I'm guessing he's not the kind of guy who likes to draw attention to himself. His brother liked the limelight. He made nothing of going up to Hunter in public or visibly tailing her anywhere. His baby brother, apparently, likes to fly under the radar. He's parked in that old rusted-out El Camino two doors down from the news van," Jay Marks pointed.

Bash spotted the outdated vehicle immediately. "Unbelievable. Has he gotten out at all?"

"He checked all the doors on the van to see if any were unlocked. He even tried to peek through the tinted windows in the back. He gave up then and went back to his car. That was forty minutes ago."

He was waiting for her. "Let's drag his ass out of there." Bash was ready.

"Not yet."

"I want him out of here before Hunter leaves the school." Bash knew they needed to get a better feel for what Jenkins wanted. *Was he stalking her exactly like his brother did? Did he want to harm her? Was he out to avenge his brother's death?* All of it sickened him. But he needed to get a grip. This was his job. Nothing like this had ever affected him before. But he had never been caught up with the woman he was trying to protect either.

"If we run him off now, there will be a next time. He will turn up and try whatever he's wanting again. We need to wait this out now and stop him in the act."

"I hear you," Bash responded, "but if he's like his next of kin, he will not miss the first time he aims and fires."

"No one was ready for that idiot that night. This is altogether different."

Bash knew he was right.

Chapter 9

Bash had no idea how much time passed, but it felt like an eternity since Hunter went inside the school. Finally, when he and Jay Marks saw her walking in between the cameraman and Bruce, Jay Marks picked up his phone. Bash watched him and listened.

"Bruce, get in the news van alone. Have Hunter stay put right there in the circle drive with the cameraman. Pick them up there promptly." Jay Marks ended the call, and then spoke to Bash. "Now we watch what Jenkins does when only Bruce gets in the van. We know he can see her now. If he moves from that car, we move." Bash nodded. Jay Marks didn't have to say it, but their weapons would be drawn the second Jenkins made any attempt to get out of his car.

When Bruce backed out the van, parked just two spots from the El Camino, both Jay Marks and Bash watched Jenkins do absolutely nothing. He had not even turned over the engine of his own vehicle. Once Hunter and the cameraman were in the news van, it drove off.

"That's it? Damn it!" Jay Marks cursed.

"We've got nothing on him." Bash was disappointed, but relieved that Hunter was safe and on her way back to the studio. His phone had alerted him twice with two separate texts from Hunter.

Are you still on the school grounds?

What's going on?

Bash had not replied.

"Let's go rattle him," Jay Marks stated, and they both stepped out of the truck. "We'll do an unofficial search of his vehicle at least. Maybe that will give us some insight to what he may have had planned today." On foot, they made their way to Jenkins, who was slouched down behind the steering wheel.

Jay Marks tapped on the closed window, and Jenkins looked up at him. He didn't seem surprised to see them there. "Step out of the car," Jay ordered him. Jenkins seemed dazed and he took his time moving.

"What are you doing here?" Bash chimed in. Both of them stood facing Jenkins, whose back was to his open car door. His hands currently were free of any weapons.

"Just watching the show," Jenkins replied, giving them both fleeting eye contact.

"Near the news van?" Jay Marks asked.

"I was hoping for that autograph I never got," he stated, and he patted the breast pocket on his denim button down shirt. There was a Sharpie visible from the top of the pocket. Bash cautiously reached for it, and plucked it out of his pocket. He dropped it into a plastic bag and sealed it before he put it into the rear pocket of his own denim. Running a check on that useless marker seemed like a waste of time, but he'd do it. Sometimes thugs attempted odd things in the most unusual ways.

"We'd like to check out what other things you have with you today," Jay Marks said, physically bumping Jenkins aside so he could sit down in the driver's seat and search his car. Bash stayed close to their person of interest outside the car.

After Jay Marks searched the front seat of that coupe utility vehicle from the late 70s, he also looked in the cargo bed before he eventually slammed both of the doors shut. "Nothing," he said, now putting his hands on Jenkins to frisk him for weapons. Jenkins cooperated, but not without wearing a smirk on his face.

"So you showed up just with your Sharpie today, huh?" Jay Marks asked him.

"You've got nothing on me, nothing to take me in for! It's a free country. I can be here, or anywhere I want. And what are you two anyway, the police? FBI?" Jenkins spat at them. He had the upper hand now, or so he thought. They both ignored his rant. Bash did carry a badge, part-time, for the Detroit Police Department. They, however, did not have a warrant for this car search. *But what did a nineteen-year-old troubled kid know about the law?*

"It's a free country for those who abide by the law. Keep it that way. Stay away from her." Bash spoke and glared at him. He came across as calm on the exterior, but his thoughts were uneasy as he was highly concerned for Hunter. And he knew he had some explaining to do to her once he replied to her texts. But there wasn't much to tell. Jenkins had followed her, and was watching her, and then waiting for her. And Bash certainly didn't want to frighten her with that information.

¥¥¥

Hunter was distracted, and she was short tempered with everyone who approached her at the studio. Bash was not answering her texts, and neither was Jay Marks. She found herself feeling seriously pissed at them both — but worried that something dire was going on.

She finally fell into a groove, researching for an upcoming interview, and that's when Jay Marks called her.

Hunter skipped a greeting and immediately started talking when she answered his call. "Well it's about damn time! It only takes a few seconds to respond to a text. It's called common courtesy."

"Save the bitching for someone else," Jay Marks always told her like it was. Sure, he worked for her, but he didn't answer to anyone.

"Are you and Bash safe?" she quickly softened. Her question revealed so much about her. Hunter was still incredibly traumatized by her brutal and heartbreaking loss. She truly did fear something happening to her people more than to herself.

"We are," Jay Marks assured her. "Jenkins was in the parking lot this morning." Hunter felt her heart rate quicken. The name Jenkins would forever bring on the same reaction for her. *Panic. Hatred.* "He pretty much stayed put in his car, parked very near the news van."

"What do you mean 'pretty much?'" Hunter wanted to know every single detail.

"I watched him the whole time. He got out and checked the doors on the van and tried looking through the back windows."

"So, he was still in his car when we were headed out to the van," Hunter gathered, "which was why you wanted me far from him."

"Yes, and once you were safe and on your way back to the studio, Bash and I approached him, got him out of the car, and checked around to see if he was armed or clearly plotting something. Nothing. We got nothing." Hunter didn't know if she should feel as relieved as she did, considering that Jay Marks sounded disappointed coming up empty-handed, but she was breathing easier knowing he didn't have a loaded gun. "He continues to carry that damn Sharpie with him, saying all he's after is an autograph."

"I'm not going near him for that," Hunter stated in disgust.

"Right. Listen, we've got your back. Just do what you do. We're watching."

"That oddly brings me comfort," Hunter told him before he ended their call.

"Good. Now get back to work."

Hunter sat in front of her laptop, thinking. She loved and trusted Jay Marks for many reasons. He was her best friend's devoted husband and the father of her children. She wouldn't allow herself yet to think of him, and all of them, without Aggie one day. Now she only wanted to focus on the fact that no one better could be in charge of her security team. Not even Bash.

And she was still miffed at him, by the way.

¥¥¥

"We have something," Bash barreled through the door and caught Jay Marks' attention. He was talking on his cell phone, and abruptly ended the call for Bash. He had been expecting this. The lab results from the Sharpie in Jenkins' pocket were already in and conclusive. "It's fentanyl."

"Shit," was Jay Mark's only response.

"We are going to bring that asshole in. I've already talked to the boys at the department. They have a warrant for his arrest." Bash was afraid for Hunter now. To think of what could have happened if she touched that Sharpie, which was precisely what Jenkins was after twice now with his ridiculous claim for an autograph, was alarming. Just absorbing that narcotic through the skin was dangerous. There was a high risk for addiction and dependence, but it could also cause respiratory distress or even death.

Jay Marks nodded in agreement. "I'm not sure how much would do immediate harm. From my knowledge, it would take more than a dusting on a pen to seriously affect someone. Am I right?"

Bash had already asked that question to the lab technician for the Detroit Police Department. "It would have to be a high dosage, but when the smallest amount is combined with other substances —like alcohol— the risks are crazy."

"Oh Christ," Jay Marks sighed. "He knows her well, doesn't he?" He was referring to Hunter's frequent drinking habit.

"She's very public. She makes no big deal of going out, even by herself, for a drink or two, or more. Standby is her go-to spot. I was there with her. Look, I'm not judging her. But the fact that she likes to tie one on could have gotten her killed with this idiot's plan to get her to touch a Sharpie with opioid residue sprinkled all over it."

Jay Marks shook his head. "Are you going to tell her, or am I?"

"I'm going to her estate now."

"Make sure she stays in. No bars. No public outings until Jenkins is locked up."

Chapter 10

She let him in, but she didn't look happy to see him. He could tell she was already in after-work mode. Alone again, she needed to take the edges off the day. She held a full glass of wine. Black leggings shaped her every curve. And a little boxy white halter t-shirt with a plunging v-neckline left very little to his imagination as she was braless. In her defense, Hunter wasn't expecting company. But Bash doubted that would have mattered.

"I typically respond to texts in a timely fashion," he began in his own defense because he knew she was thinking it. And probably stewing about his lack of communication. Jay Marks had followed up with her, but he hadn't. Bash had his reasons, and he was at her home now because he believed she deserved to be told something like this in person. He didn't want to put any kind of fear in her, but they had proof that she was being targeted by the man whose brother killed her fiancé. Another unstable fan.

"Can I get you a drink?" she asked him, as she moved out of the foyer where they already had the tendency to linger.

"No, I'm fine," Bash answered and he watched her walk over to one of the ivory sofas. She sat in the center of it, took a generous sip of wine, and looked up at him again.

"You can sit," she offered.

"I need to be on my feet for this," he said, without an explanation. When he was nervous or had an argument to defend or a point to make, he stood. And sometimes paced. "I believe Jay told you that we didn't have anything on Jenkins to hold him."

"I know that he snooped around our news van, while he was apparently waiting for me. But he didn't have a weapon," *Thank God,* she thought, but didn't verbalize it.

"He wanted your autograph again," Bash told her, but that wasn't new information, as Jay Marks already mentioned it. "I confiscated the Sharpie in his shirt pocket because I wondered if it was worth testing it. I didn't expect anything conclusive to turn up."

Hunter stopped sipping her wine, and set it down on the glass-top coffee table directly in front of her. "But, something did?"

"Fentanyl," he answered her and it was almost as if he could see the wheels turning in her mind.

"There was a story awhile back about narcotic residue being left on grocery carts. The police warned people of it, and advised everyone to use the sanitizer wipes to clean off the handle of their cart before putting their hands on it." Bash should have known that Hunter was educated on endless topics. She was the news. She knew current events. "But they later released a statement downplaying the danger of it. Could there really have been enough Fentanyl on that marker to endanger me somehow?" She was still in reporter mode, as Bash noticed she did not seem alarmed. She was only searching for knowledge.

"That's the question," Bash stated. "Just absorbing it through the skin is dangerous, and especially if it comes into contact with your nose or eyes. There's a high risk then for addiction and dependence, and it could also cause respiratory distress or even death."

"But again, it would have to be a high dosage to be that serious." It appeared as if Hunter wanted to be reassured.

"The concern here is that when the smallest amount is combined with other substances —like alcohol— the risks can be crazy." Bash awaited her response.

Hunter sat there for a moment. She actually smirked first, before she responded. "Here we go again, huh? Someone is stalking me to the point of knowing too much about me."

"I'll be honest, I said earlier that you are very public. People see you at Standby, they know you like to have a few drinks to unwind or have a good time. You're going to have to check yourself for awhile, and be more careful."

"If you have proof that Jimmy Jenkins tried to drug me, then he's in police custody, right?" Hunter asked him. "I've told you before, I am not going to live in fear. That's why I have cameras all over this place and a security team to keep me safe, 24/7."

Bash hesitated. "I'm waiting to hear that they have him. There's a warrant out for his arrest. This all just happened before I came over here."

Hunter nodded, believing it was just a matter of time then, and she reached for her glass of wine. She definitely wasn't the type of woman to freak out. Or maybe she just concealed her feelings well.

"Thank you," Hunter said to him. "Would you like to sit down now?"

He smiled at her. "Tell me why you're thanking me?" He walked over to the sofa and sat beside her.

"You made a house call. You're here, telling me what's going on when you could have just used your phone."

Bash reached for her knee, and his entire hand swallowed it up and then some. "I told you, I want to be here for you. I'll do everything possible to keep you safe." Hunter turned to him and he leaned in to her.

"Do you want to get some dinner or something?" she asked him. She enjoyed spending time with him, and having him sit close to her on the sofa. It felt nice to have someone there. To have Bash there.

"As in go out? Have you not heard a word a said?" he chuckled, and then shook his head.

"I thought I was safe with you?" she teased him. "We could choose carry-out food from anywhere you'd like if you want to stay in this big, lonely house with me."

"You *are* safe with me," he reassured her, "and I do like the idea of take-out food in this big house. But it's not lonely when you have someone sitting beside you. Someone who wants to be here, regardless of his job description."

Hunter leaned in to him and initiated the kiss that began as soft and gentle, and fiery and passionate, all at once. The desire to deepen their kiss escalated quickly between them. Hunter ran her hands through the back of his dark hair, while Bash had his hands on her face and jawline and neck and then lower. He felt her bare breasts through that thin t-shirt she wore so well. She whimpered beneath his touch and that sensual sound alone sent him reeling. He could get lost in her, for sure. She untucked his t-shirt from the front of his denim and she started to reach for the button and zipper. "Damn it… the cameras," she whispered, just as Bash's phone rang in his rear pocket.

"And, damn it, my phone," he groaned.

He reached for it and answered immediately.

"I'm not going to sit here and watch this porn." It was Jay Marks, who laughed first, and then got right to the point of why he called. "The police went to Jenkins' apartment and he's gone. His girlfriend said he packed a bag and left this morning. He's running."

"Wonderful," Bash spoke regretfully into the phone, and Hunter creased her brow. She knew it was Jay Marks' voice on the opposite end of that phone, but she couldn't hear the words he said. "Well he's young, and probably has no money. He's going to have to stop for work. We'll track him."

"That's exactly what I said, but for tonight we need Hunter well protected. I don't want her alone in that house, and from the looks of the camera feed you might have that covered."

"Pervert." Bash spoke and rolled his eyes, and Hunter muffled her laughter with her hand over her mouth. She knew they had been seen. She couldn't have cared less though. She wanted this man. *Tonight.*

"I'm going home," Jay Marks informed him. "Just stay there with her. Jackson will be around to check the feed after midnight. Other than that, she's all yours." Bash did like the sound of that, but convincing Hunter to let him stay was going to be a battle.

Chapter 11

"What's going on?" Hunter asked, the moment Bash ended the phone call.

"Jenkins apparently fled this morning. The police went to his apartment and only found his girlfriend who admitted he packed up and left."

"I hope he keeps running," Hunter stated.

"He needs to be caught, and suffer the consequences of his stupidity," Bash disagreed with her.

"That too, but at least he's far away from me." Hunter did feel relieved.

"We don't know that for sure," Bash argued again. "He could be staked out somewhere near this estate, trying to figure out how to get on the grounds, unnoticed."

"Are you purposely trying to put that fear in me?"

"No, of course not. But we have to be realistic. He's dangerous. Given that fact, I just received orders from Jay to stay here with you tonight. It's precautionary."

Hunter's eyes widened. *That wasn't really going to happen. It couldn't. Well, there were guest rooms…*

"I don't think that's necessary," she began, not knowing how else to address this.

"Actually it is essential," he told her. "No pressure, though. Let's just have dinner and I will stay down here on one of these comfy sofas tonight."

No pressure? Did he feel the budding sexual tension between them? The weight of it had already left her breathless.

"Dinner can be your choice," she reminded him. "Whether or not you stay here all night is mine." Bash was initially right. This was definitely going to be a battle with her.

¥¥¥

They ordered pizza. Bash insisted on meeting the delivery guy outside of the gate. When he returned to the house with their pizza, Hunter had plates set on the coffee table and a longneck bottle of beer for Bash. She refilled her wine glass.

"Pizza and beer. A guy's dream," Bash grinned as he sat down on the floor near the coffee table and flipped open the lid on the pizza box.

"You're easy then," she giggled, as she made her way to the floor also. She took the first slice and stretched the cheese from her lips before chewing. *"Mm… God this is good."*

Bash felt himself tighten between his legs. *Yeah, it certainly was this guy's dream.*

He drank a second beer when Hunter refilled her wine glass for the third time. They sat on the floor together long after they were finished eating. For awhile, they shared silence. Music played almost all the time over the speaker system throughout the entire house.

"This is nice," she admitted to him, and he turned to look at her. They were sitting close but not touching. "I don't want any expectations, Bash. I can't, okay?"

"Expectations," he repeated her word choice. "So, that's your way of getting into my pants, but not committing to courting me."

She giggled. "I'm such a man."

"I guess that makes me the lady?" he commented, and they both laughed. And then Bash spoke again, seriously this time. "I think we both know we can plan our lives all we want, but nothing goes according to protocol. Just like that, it can all be gone. While I've learned to live for the moment, I've also recognized the importance of seizing happiness."

"I can't believe I am going to share this with you," Hunter said, feeling compelled to connect with him on a deeper level after what he had just said. "Aggie accused me of getting too comfortable in my pain. She said I've forgotten how to be happy."

"I'm on Aggie's side," Bash smiled and blinked his eyes a few times, which made him look both boyish and sexy. "Absolutely, she's right. You free-fell into a pit of grief and loneliness, and you're allowing it to trap you there. I've got the rope, sweetheart, just grab ahold of it and I'll pull you up and out of there. Happiness should be sought after and fought for."

"How do you do that when you've been through it, too? I don't understand." Hunter was being bare bones honest.

"No, I guess you really don't. You can't see that I found my reason to be happy. I want to move on from the pain. My need to be completely fulfilled and happy again must be greater than yours."

He had the greater need.

That truth, that realization absolutely stunned her. Hunter had never met anyone else like him. She did want Bash, more than just physically, and she knew how much she could begin to need him in her life. Everything had already felt different and better with him around her. But she wondered when she would ever stop fighting herself, or holding on too tightly to Cooper's memory.

"I don't even know what to say to that," she admitted. "I can't just flip a switch and change my mindset. I'm not the same person I was before. Losing Cooper, having the blueprint for my future shredded before my eyes, changed me."

"Me too," Bash agreed. "My wife went to work one day, and never came home. Did she know how much I loved her, and truly needed her? I never got to say goodbye. That alone can eat away at a person's soul."

Hunter thought of lying on the cold ground with Cooper, in the last moments of his life. They did say goodbye, but it was a brutally sudden and forced farewell that broke her heart in half. "I hear you," was all she said to Bash right now. She really had not found closure with Cooper either. Not in that moment when he took his last breath with her by his side, and then her entire world unraveled.

"Good," he responded, and he reached for and touched her hand. She intertwined her fingers with his. "That's all I can ask. Just hear me. Be open to the idea of finding your happiness."

Their faces were only inches apart. She moved to lay her head on his chest. She could hear his heart beating. She closed her eyes then, while he wrapped her in his strong, comforting arms and held her.

¥¥¥

In the moment, Hunter knew exactly what she was doing. She also felt so content in his arms while drifting off to the most rested state of sleep she had experienced in a very long time. So that's where she stayed all night long. On the floor in her massive living room, in Bash's arms.

Half of her body was draped across his chest and his stomach when she opened her eyes. He was already awake. He had not slept much at all. His was alert to his surroundings, and had checked his phone probably too often. It had been quiet at the estate and Hunter was safe and sound in his arms. That was likely another reason why Bash had not been able to drift off to sleep. He wanted to savor every single second of being that close to her.

"Good morning," Bash gently touched her cheek with the palm of his hand.

Hunter only stared at him for a moment, as the sleep was still in her eyes. *It was morning. He had stayed for the sunrise.* "What time is it?" she heard the panic in her own voice. *She had to be at the studio!*

"It's five, you have time," he read her mind.

"I usually workout before I shower. I need to be in makeup by 7, and hair after that."

Bash smiled. "What any woman wouldn't give to state it that way. It's like being pampered every day."

"It's more than that," she wanted to clarify. "I work hard." *The pampering was part of the gig.* Hunter was obviously upset, but it had nothing to do with her career or the provided hair and makeup perk. It was a ridiculous argument which stemmed from Hunter being upset with herself. *Bash should have gone home last night. They never had sex. He never left.* And she was angry with herself for allowing herself to feel so at ease with him all night long. This was not what she did. She was teetering on the verge of something she had sworn off.

Bash stood up when Hunter did. "Go get ready and I'll drive you to the studio."

"I have Jackson for that," she stated as a matter of fact.

"I'm filling in for him this morning."

Hunter rolled her eyes, and stormed up the stairs.

Bash just stood there and watched her. He knew she was a handful, and getting her to fully commit to him would likely be one the most difficult missions he's had yet. She was beyond headstrong, and adamant about keeping up those walls around her heart. But Bash was certain she would be worth the fight. The fact that she challenged him was something else he already loved about her too.

Chapter 12

Hunter was already in the hair chair before Aggie was waiting for her. That never happened. She instantly worried that Aggie wasn't feeling well this morning. Hunter had been so wrapped up in her own craziness, that she allowed checking in with her go by the wayside. Just as Hunter was about to get up and go search for her, Aggie made her way backstage.

"Hey, you okay?" Hunter spoke first.

"Yeah, just needed a potty break," Aggie explained, but Hunter could see she was wincing in pain from something. Her walk looked different. It was as if one leg was being slightly dragged. Nothing overly noticeable, but Hunter caught it. The intercom blared above them, announcing an impromptu staff meeting in thirty minutes. Hunter turned in her chair and her eyes were as wide as Aggie's. They were going to be pressed for time.

"I'm just straightening it super quick then," Aggie referred to Hunter's hair. She nodded. They needed to hurry, as she still had to get to wardrobe before that meeting. "Just talk to me really fast while I do this."

"About what?"

"We don't have time for you to fake your innocence. What happened with you and Bash last night?"

"Why don't you just have your husband play back the footage for you."

"Did you do it? You slept with him?" Aggie seemed thrilled at the thought.

"He stayed with me all night to protect me. No sex happened."

"I'm surprised, and a little impressed by your self control," Aggie stated, with a giggle.

"Shut up," Hunter all but spat at her.

"What's going on with you?"

"Just hurry and do my hair," Hunter spoke rudely, and instantly felt guilty because *what if Aggie was suffering this morning and could not make her hands cooperate to work in a speedy fashion?*

"Hey," Aggie caught her eye in the mirror. "It's me you're talking to. Can't run. Can't hide. So you may as well just tell me."

Hunter kept her voice low. "I fell asleep in his arms on my living room floor after we ate pizza and drank a little alcohol. I haven't felt so at peace in a very long time," she paused, as Aggie's face lit up, "and now I'm so pissed at myself because the gravitational pull toward him almost feels as if it's out of my control."

Aggie let out a little squeal in celebration, but Hunter chose to ignore her. "When are you going to realize that it most definitely is very much out of your control? So, accept it, and just stop fighting it."

Hunter didn't believe she could do that.

¥¥¥

Bruce was not on time to the staff meeting that he requested. Someone remarked how unlike him that was, just as he hustled through the door. "I'm late!" he announced, "so I guess there really is a first time for everything." Laughter from a few of the staff filled the conference room, as they all watched their producer refrain from taking a seat at the long rectangular-shaped table. He stood there in a gray three-piece suit, sans a tie. Not a single thick silver hair was out of place on his head. Hunter never took her eyes off of him. She loved and admired and respected that man like a father.

"We have limited time, so let me just state what's happening after the newscast this morning." That pertained to Hunter. Her live interview aired then. "And this has everything to do with our ratings. We are on top, yes, but we have some damn good competition. I fell into a way to spike our numbers this week, and I feel strongly about it. So, I want no objections." Bruce looked at Hunter. She remained expressionless. "The script has changed for this morning. We are not going live with the scheduled interview." Hunter worked well under pressure. She didn't flinch. The interview on college debt with several college students would have to wait. Even though she had done her research and was well prepared, it would be sidelined. She trusted Bruce. He could smell a good news story. She was going to have to scramble to throw together what Bruce wanted, but this was not the first time. She thought she would welcome the challenge this morning — until Bruce revealed what it was.

"The latest rave in publication is a book written by Thomas Zahn," Hunter inhaled a slow, deep breath. She was aware. The book was a New York Times Bestseller for the third consecutive week. Aggie was all about reading anything she could get her hands on, and she had practically begged Hunter to crack it open. That book was on the nightstand beside her bed. She had yet to give it a chance, as Aggie pleaded. Hunter didn't believe in self help for grievers. The title of the book, "Approval to Carry On," now rolled off of Bruce's tongue.

"Zahn was at the same coffeehouse as I was this morning. I booked the interview, Hunter. You're on with him in twenty-two minutes." Hunter again remained expressionless. Other than a nod in her producer's direction, she stayed silent. Bruce adjourned the meeting and Hunter stayed. She had something to say.

"This book certainly seems to be the rave. I need to run out of here and do some quick research so I don't look like I have my head up my ass when Mr. Zahn is waiting for me to take the lead."

"Wait," Bruce stopped her, standing directly in front of him. He felt a tremendous weight of guilt. These types of interviews were typically ones that he repeatedly asked Hunter if she was comfortable with. For this one, time wasn't a luxury they had. "I know what I'm doing by expecting this of you. It's a subject that's very personal for you, I see that, but you have the tendency to become someone else on camera. You're the strongest professional in this business. We need to be the first to snag this interview. I apologize if it feels like I'm disrespecting you in any way."

"Business trumps feelings," Hunter stated, and she felt anxious to get moving so she could prepare herself for an interview that was going to sit idle in the pit of her stomach for days.

¥¥¥

It didn't help her nerves that she saw Bash, showered and changed, and loitering offstage just as she took her place in front of the cameras. She glanced at him and then quickly looked away before he saw her looking at him. He would be a distraction if she didn't just ignore the fact that he was there, and watching the broadcast. She wondered if something new had come up with Jenkins. Why else had he showed up at the studio after already having dropped her off this morning? Their fifteen-minute car ride there consisted of very little small talk and mostly shared silence. Hunter halted her thoughts as the production assistant was escorting the best-selling author toward her now. *Ready or not.*

Any other time, she would have done her homework in its entirety by reading the book front to back. She silently cursed herself for not listening to Aggie. *Why did she always have to be right? Know-it-all.*

Hunter had taken ten minutes, max, to read the synopsis of the book, "Approval to Carry On," and she had her questions ready. She was honestly prepared in a half-assed way. She could improvise and everybody would just move on. Or she could nail it, and the network's ratings would soar. She knew what she should do. Bruce always commended her for her courage. She hoped she could again make him proud, but this time that meant she would have to allow herself to be vulnerable. She was in the public eye, but she had kept silent about so much of her life in the past three years. For the ratings, she contemplated opening up about her personal story. That was, if she didn't back out and just end up winging a feature story that barely tugged at the heartstrings of the viewers. *The ratings!* Hunter mentally reminded herself. No other network had yet interviewed this author, and this one had a newscaster who could truly benefit from reading this book. Hunter was taking Aggie's word for that.

What Hunter knew for certain was that Thomas Zahn wrote the book, "Approval to Carry On," after he had experienced personal loss. Within a twenty-year span, he and his wife lost an infant daughter, Thomas's wife died unexpectedly, and lastly his teenage son also died. Loss was huge for this man. So immense that Hunter questioned how he could ever take the steps to move on, much less write an inspirational book about it. In the book's synopsis, the author stated that *the person who grieves determines whether or not they want to heal.* He claimed in his writing that there was *a new way to handle grief,* and that he could teach readers how. Hunter was skeptical of it, and of him, but a part of her was also curious. And maybe even hopeful.

Chapter 13

The clustered studio lights were hot above them. The cameras were rolling. The production team was counting on her. She felt at ease, like always, as she began her segment.

"I want to welcome Thomas Zahn to ABS NewsChannel 7 this morning. We are honored to have you join us," Hunter was charismatic on camera, and in person, and the middle-aged man seated with her now for this interview, was very taken by her. "I do have a confession to make. Your arrival to our studio this morning was not preplanned, and this interview was just sprung on me about an hour ago — so I am in the minority when I confess that I have yet to read your book, 'Approval to Carry On.' I do have a copy on my nightstand in my bedroom. Very good intentions on my part, but I'll blame my hectic schedule on not yet finding the time to read." Hunter imagined Aggie rolling her eyes backstage. *Liar. You'll say anything to enhance the story.* Bash stood backstage, watching and listening, and he momentarily naughtily focused on the mention of her bedroom. One day, they would share a bed. He didn't just want her body. He was confident in his budding love for her. "I would like to begin by having you share with our readers why you wrote this book. I know your followers and our viewers already are aware of your personal grief. You lost your infant daughter, your wife, and your teenage son, all within two decades of your life. So many hearts break for you, and I know I speak for everyone when I say that I cannot fathom how you have carried on."

Thomas Zahn confidently took the lead to answer Hunter's question. "I was stuck in unimaginable grief. I allowed myself to be there. I needed to be there. We all do. Grieving and mourning those we loved and lost is a natural, painful process that takes time. What is not natural or healthy is to stay there forever. I had to find a way to climb out of the sadness. Writing was an outlet for me. Helping others eventually became a mission for me. Time hasn't healed me, but identifying how I was causing myself more pain by sinking in limbo and not carrying on, was what did."

Hunter reminded herself to focus. This man, this successful author, probably had answered that very same question in a hundred other print interviews thus far. This first, live, television interview was going to be predictable, and perhaps even boring. Hunter Raine wasn't typical at anything. And it was time she proved that again. She needed to take this story, her story with a best-selling author this morning, to the next level. Detroit loved her. She was their number one newswoman. It was time she showed them a piece of her pain. And, in turn, she would put a man who survived grief in the limelight. *Could he genuinely help her heal as well?*

Hunter took the lead again.

"Three years ago, I was less than a week away from becoming Mrs. Aaron Cooper," her voice caught. *Had she ever said that out loud before?* The team in that studio, behind the cameras and backstage, all wore expressions of sheer shock. Aggie felt her eyes tear up. Bash inhaled a slow breath through his nostrils. "I never got married because a gunman, a stalker fan, took my fiancé's life. I have my career and I have my close circle of friends and family who have kept my head above water, but I'm admitting to myself and all of Detroit this morning that I have not healed. And I have not carried on because I don't know how to. Or maybe, if I'm being truly honest, I refuse to allow myself to carry on without the man who completed me." Hunter's voice was strong, but her hands were trembling. The viewers watched author Thomas Zahn lean forward in his armchair to take her hand in his to offer her comfort. He understood her pain and her grief, and most importantly her unwillingness to move forward.

"That took a tremendous amount of courage, Hunter," he told her and the live audience watching, most likely with dropped jaws and wide eyes. "You may not realize it, but you've taken the first step already, just now. With such grace, you admitted very publicly that you want to live again. I'm inspired by you."

Hunter smiled, sincerely. "So where do I go from here? Because the pain still feels the same. The resistance to love again feels just as strong." Bash never took his eyes off of her. He wondered if this was partly Hunter Raine the journalist seeking higher ratings, or if she was being sincere.

"One day at a time will get you there," the author told her. "Listen to the voice inside you that wants to live again, as opposed to the one that's reminding you of your tragic loss and preventing you from moving on. It's important, in all of us, that we choose the greater need. Happiness over sorrow."

Hunter was momentarily speechless. She was taken aback by his words. *The greater need.* It was something she understood extremely well. The camera panned close. In her ear monitor, she heard Bruce speak directly to her for the first time since they went live. He didn't preach his typical lines. *Commercial in thirty seconds. Stretch time. That's a wrap.* This time, he said, "Keep going girl." She knew that not only meant they were stretching the segment and not transitioning to the commercial break, but it also was her mentor's way of encouraging her to stay on task. *He approved. He was proud.*

She could almost hear him say*, The audience will love this. And you, even more.*

She waved a hand in front of her face, in an effort to pause and excuse her tears. And then she finally found her voice again. "I suppose I should crack open that book of yours," she teased, because in order to regain her composure she needed to find the humor right now, and get a chuckle out of someone. Thomas Zahn did laugh. "Your spoken words obviously affected me this morning, and I thank you sincerely from my heart, for that, and for joining all of us here at ABS News today."

"Absolutely," he replied, and the camera abruptly panned out as this inspiring author unexpectedly stood up to open his arms to Hunter. This was completely off-script for her. She wasn't a hugger, and rarely on-air did she ever. But this time, on cue, she followed her subject's lead. And the two of them warmly embraced. Ultimately, there were very few dry eyes in the studio.

And in her ear monitor, Hunter heard, "*That's a wrap.*"

¥¥¥

She spoke to Thomas Zahn for a few additional minutes once they were off the air. The studio remained unusually quiet. As they parted, Hunter stood on set and unclipped the tiny microphone on her chest, in the v of her dress. Bruce was the first one to approach her. She looked up at him, because even in high heels, he was a tall man next to her. He shook his head back and forth and met her eyes with his. Hunter saw pride beaming in those hazel eyes. "So, was that foolish of me, or brilliant?" she asked him, attempting to make light of how truly genuine she had been on camera. Bruce smiled wide, and he winked at her. "You were wonderful. Go on and tell yourself that you did it for the ratings, but I won't completely buy it. Not this time." He leaned forward and kissed her on the cheek. Hunter felt like a little girl on the receiving end of a father's adoration. Bruce walked away before he broke down. Hunter, in turn, was so moved by his reaction, that she choked up again. And before she could bolt out of there to her office, Aggie pulled her into her arms. "I love you so much. Don't you dare tell me it was an act, or I'll beat your ass in front of everyone." They giggled through their suppressed tears.

And finally, Hunter saw him. Bash was a few feet from her. He closed the space between them then, but he never reached for her or touched her. He kept his voice low. "You are an amazing journalist, and an incredible woman. Beautiful, inside and out. And I'm falling in love with you." She was looking up at him, and she quickly dropped her chin and ceased eye contact. He lifted her head gently by her chin with two of his fingers, and she didn't know what to say. "It's okay," he said, as if he was reassuring her that she didn't have to say it back, or anything at all to him right now. "I just wanted you to know."

Chapter 14

Jay Marks had taken the morning off work, and once Aggie finished styling everyone's hair at the studio, he picked her up there for her doctor's appointment with a specialist. This one was a neurologist.

When the two of them left that appointment at Henry Ford Hospital in Detroit, Aggie asked to sit down outside on one of the backless concrete benches on the grounds. Her husband immediately assumed she was worn out and needed to rest, even though he had not seen any sign of that. She appeared strong today, and had even said as much to the doctor.

It was everything the doctor had said to Aggie that was weighing on her mind.

The life expectancy of a person with ALS averages about two to five years from the time of diagnosis. This disease, however, is variable, and many people can live longer than that. More than half live longer than three years.

Once ALS starts, it almost always progresses, eventually taking away the ability to walk, dress, write, speak, swallow, and breathe easily — all of which will shorten a lifespan.

How quickly, and in which order, was different from person to person, Aggie remembered hearing the neurologist say. *And the progression was not always going to be steady. She could have weeks or months of lasting time where there was very little loss or no loss of any functions.*

There would be more specialists to enter her life. Not just the neurologist that she met today. A speech therapist was essential to help her communicate, an occupational therapist would improve the daily skills that she will gradually lose, a pulmonologist who treated respiratory tract disease, and there would be an abundance of palliative medicine needed to attempt to improve or sustain her quality of life.

"You okay?" he asked her, sitting down beside her, and he rubbed her knee with his large hand. Jay Marks was a big, muscular man with not a hair on his head or stubble on his face. Aggie saw the sadness in his blue eyes right now.

"I am okay," she told him, honestly. "Other than my hands stiffening up a little more lately, I feel good. I still feel normal, Jay." He wondered if she didn't realize that she slightly dragged her left leg the past few days. *Maybe she thought he hadn't noticed?*

"Good," he said to her with a soft smile. "So would you like to grab an early lunch?"

"I would," she answered, "but in a minute." He watched her move her dark wire rimmed glasses higher on her nose. Her equally as dark eyes behind those rims looked bright and healthy. Her black long hair was pulled up high on her head again today. Loose hairs sprouted from the top of that messy bun. She was a striking woman. She carried excess weight from both of her pregnancies, but Jay preferred to have a handful of a woman in his arms. The thought of her being so very sick and losing every function imaginable — eventually dwindling her body down to being useless and weak and weary — depleted his spirit. He knew he had to think positive and be strong for his wife and their sons, but this devastated him beyond any optimism or faith.

"Hear me out," she continued. "I think you know how proud I am. Proud of all I've accomplished and everything that I have. I'm a cosmetologist at a television studio, I am your wife, and I am a mother of two beautiful little boys. I am so gratified by it all. I've had thirty-three years of a really good life. But, that's about to change." Jay wanted to take her hand, but he refrained from even slightly moving as he allowed her to continue speaking. His wife was a fighter. But she was also a realist. She accepted the things that could not be changed. "I will lose the use of my hands and that will take away my gift of doing hair. My mobility will be gone, so taking care of two rambunctious boys and playing and living day to day with them will be no more. I will not even be able to read to them as my voice will also fade. Everything I am able to be to you as your wife will die out and I will be a useless woman to you." Jay shook his head no, but she kept speaking and she even spoke for him. "I know you will want to take care of me, and I love you even more for that. But I can't watch you or the boys pity me. I won't."

He suddenly felt panicked. He knew his wife extremely well. She harbored profound thoughts, and always had a plan. She wore the look on her face now that he knew all too well. Her mind was made up. "We made vows," he finally spoke to her. "For better or worse, in sickness and in health…"

"Jay," she spoke his name and it unexpectedly brought tears to his eyes. "I need you to support me on this. Please. No arguments. Just spend my last days with me and our boys and let's do things together and smile and laugh and make memories to last you and them long after I'm gone. Oh, and take pictures. We will take lots of pictures."

"We can do that," he nodded his head, and a tear escaped down his cheek. Aggie used her fingers to wipe it away.

"And when my body begins to fail me," she spoke slow, to be sure she had all of his attention, "I want you to help me leave this world with my dignity."

Jay shook his head adamantly. "Oh God, Ags, no. Come on, you cannot be serious? No. What are you doing? Don't take yourself there. You are so strong, you're my fighter. I will give you my strength too. Please, no."

Aggie had tears streaming down her face. "No. I will not change my mind. I want to die feeling whole. I want the boys' last memory of me to be of a woman they loved and respected and admired. Not an invalid who withered away to nothing."

Jay understood more than he wanted to admit, and he tried his best to convey that to her. "I know I would feel the very same way. Believe me, I would," he paused to take a deep breath. "But, I can't help you take your life. How would I live with myself knowing that I took you away from our boys? That I shortchanged them of their time they had left with their mommy?"

"The disease is going to take me away from them. Not you. Just help me. Do this for me, and with me. Hold my hand," she paused, in search of all right words to reach him, and convince him. "You heard the doctor, I could have years left yet. I'm not asking you to do it after lunch today. Just when the time comes, Jay. Please."

He shook his head and stood up. He paced a few times in front of her on the bench, with his hands in the front pockets of his denim. And then, when he stopped, he finally turned to her. He pulled her up to her feet by her hands. And then he spoke. "I don't like what you want to do. I hate what you're saying and how you are planning ahead to do it. But, I understand. I just can't be the one to help you. I think you know who can though."

Aggie creased her brow, but the wheels in her mind didn't have to search for this at all. She already knew. "Hunter…" she spoke in barely a whisper, and her husband pulled her into his arms and held her. He didn't agree with her choice, but he understood. And they both believed Hunter inevitably would too.

Chapter 15

Aggie insisted on going to see Hunter alone. She compromised and let Jackson drive her to the estate once she knew that Hunter was home from the television studio.

Hunter's cell phone sent an alert to inform her that Jackson had entered the gate. She was upstairs in her bedroom, and had just changed into a pair of skinny, destressed jeans with a scoopneck black sweater. She wore a lacy white halter bralette underneath. She moved quickly down the stairs in her bare feet to get to the door in time for Jackson to park in the circle drive. Hunter assumed there was some confusion, as she was not going out. *Not yet. Maybe later.*

She flung open the door and stepped onto the wide-paneled flooring on the immense front porch. She watched Jackson roll down the passenger side window of his black SUV. "I have a delivery for you," he yelled up to her.

"Oh?" she asked him.

And, with that, the back door of the SUV opened up and Aggie scooted out.

"Seriously! Ags!" she giggled. "Get your ass in my house. What a nice surprise." Jackson laughed at the two of them acting like girls together on the front porch, and he waited to drive off until they were both safely inside the house.

"Who said you could use my driver?" Hunter joked, and secretly hoped Aggie had not already lost trust in her own independence.

"My husband said," she giggled. "He insisted actually."

They simultaneously sat down on one of the sofas, but then Hunter started to stand again. "Can I get you a drink? Water, if you'd rather?" Hunter, of course, thought of Aggie's health and the medication she was taking, but she seriously pondered for a moment how she could not recall a time the two of them drank only water together. Maybe to curb their drunken state before driving home when they were in their young, careless, years?

"Not right now, and you either, okay?" Aggie requested. "I want you to have a clear head for this."

No. Hunter thought. *Aggie was going to tell her that her condition was worsening. Or something to that dire effect that was terribly wrong.* She waited, with a sudden increased heart rate and clammy hands, for Aggie to explain.

"I had an appointment this morning with a neurologist. He was good, but I hated his every word," Aggie admitted, and Hunter caught herself taking in a very deep breath. Oftentimes she feared life would throw something else at her that she just wouldn't have the courage or the strength or any will left to fight. And she was certain now that this was it. "I'll spare you the depressing details, and give you the cliff notes version. My life expectancy is two to five years. Once this ALS shit really kicks in, it will continuously progress and rob me of my ability to walk, bathe and dress myself, write, speak, swallow, and fucking breathe. Oh, but on the bright, sunny-ass side, I could have lengths of time where I will see little or no loss of any functions that complete me as a human being." Hunter stayed quiet, only watching Aggie's face and listening raptly. *She was angry. And she damn well had every right to be.* "Bottom line? I don't want to do this."

"And I don't blame you at all," Hunter spoke softly. "This sucks. And, if I am being completely honest, as I always am with you, I do not want to watch this happen to you. I do not want to muster up the strength to be a part of your decline," Hunter choked on her words. "You are a part of me, Ags. The best part of me. I don't even know how to breathe without you in my life — and my hair is going to look like a fucking rat's nest on camera!" There was always shared humor between the two of them. When life got too tough, and the emotions ran too high, they laughed together.

"Listen to yourself," Aggie told her. "You just said everything that I wanted to hear right now. You don't want to spend those sickening, devastating last days with me. You can't bear to watch it. Well neither can I."

Hunter was quick to defend her own words. "I didn't mean that I won't be there. I would do anything for you, Ags. You know that."

"There again, you are it for me. You are exactly what I need in my life. You always have been, Hunter. And now, at the end of my life, or when that time comes, I am asking you to again do exactly what I need."

"I don't quite understand what that all will entail, but yes, whatever it is, I will be there to help you in any way that you need."

Aggie nodded her head repeatedly and smiled warmly at her best friend. "I'm not going to let it get to that point," she admitted, and Hunter sat back on the sofa. And then she sat forward again. She was afraid to ask what that meant. "I am going to live out all the time I have left, feeling this good, like I do right now. I told Jay that I want to make more memories with the boys. As they grow into young men and then adulthood one day, I want them to always recall their mommy as strong and funny and beautiful. Not sick. Not weak. Not useless to them." Hunter now realized the urgency of Aggie's visit, following the glum and depressing news from the doctor. "Jay won't do it. He says he can't. He understands, but he can't."

Aggie watched the tears trickle down Hunter's cheeks. "What are you planning, Ags? No. Don't answer me. Just know that I choose to believe that time is going to be a long damn ways off. Okay? But, when you reach that bridge," *God, all of this was unbelievably heartbreaking for Hunter to imagine,* "I will help you jump off."

Aggie grabbed ahold of Hunter's face. She held her cheeks lovingly with her open palms. They both started to cry. Their foreheads touched. Hunter could hardly make out Aggie's words between sobs, but she did hear her say, "I love you the most."

¥¥¥

A short while after Aggie left the estate, Hunter knew that Jackson had to be on his way back downtown in an empty vehicle, so she called him. "Come by for me. I'm going out."

Jackson tried to sway her, but she insisted, so he caved. After all, he did work for her. The first person he called on the drive back to Hunter's estate was Jay Marks. He knew this wasn't going to go over well with him or Bash as they were nearly a couple hundred miles away in Cleveland, Ohio, following a lead on Jimmy Jenkins.

"She wants to go out. I assume Standby. I'm on my way to pick her up now."

"What? She's insane," Jay Marks spoke into his phone as he sat behind the wheel of his truck with Bash in the passenger seat. The lead in Cleveland had not panned out. They were still one hundred and seventy miles away from Detroit. Leaving now, they still needed two hours and forty minutes to get home. "Can you stall her?" Bash looked to the side at Jay Marks. He hadn't wanted to travel so far out from Detroit earlier today, but he did it hoping an anonymous tip would lead them to finding Jenkins. Now, he worried that Jenkins was closer to Hunter than they were.

"She's adamant," Jackson told him.

"Then go, but do not for any reason let her out of your sight. If she pees, you pee. Got it?"

"Yes, sir."

Bash felt his blood pressure rise when Jay Marks ended the call. "I want to call her and tell her to wait. Wait for me. We'll have a late dinner. Or just advise her to stay in her house, where it's safe. But, she and I are not there yet. She's a woman who wants to believe she can save herself. I don't understand the no-fear."

"She does this ridiculousness sometimes," Jay Marks attempted to explain, "she flees, she drinks, she parties, she brings a man home, whenever she's really hurting. Aggie was with her for awhile today. It's depressing shit, man. We are going to lose her. Hunter is reeling. That, I can understand." Bash heard his every word, but he hung on the fact that Hunter could turn to and have sex with another man tonight. He was hurt and angry that she had not turned to him today. Even after she appeared to have a breakthrough in her grief live on television. And especially after he declared his feelings for her.

"Can't you drive this thing any faster?" Bash barked at Jay Marks.

"I'm worried, too," was all he replied.

Neither one of them spoke it, but they both feared the dead-end lead nearly two hundred miles from Hunter had been a set up.

Chapter 16

Jackson sipped a beer at the bar, seated right beside Hunter. She didn't object to his close presence and his insistence to keep his eyes on her, but she chose to sit at the bar. She wanted to talk to more people than just her driver.

She was drinking vodka tonics tonight, and was on her third when Christian walked in. He made his way around the bar to Hunter's side. "Hey baby, you're back," he kissed her on the cheek and let his lips linger there. He was a jealous man when he heard that Hunter had been at his bar with her new bodyguard and they had been very cozy with each other in the corner booth.

"I never left," she declared. "You know this bar is, by far, my favorite in the city." Jackson recognized drunk flirting when he saw it. And he could unfortunately already foresee having to drive the both of them back to her estate later. Hunter broke free of Christian's hold first. He took a generous sip of her drink, and she playfully slapped him on the chest. "Get your own!" she told him, probably a little too loud. The weeknight crowd in there was sparse tonight though. Jackson thought everyone seemed to be minding their own business.

Christian continued to invade her personal space as he spoke something under his breath, close to Hunter's ear and she giggled.

Jackson nudged her. "Last drink, and we need to go, alright?"

"Oh… one more," she whined. "It's still early." They had been there for almost two hours, and Jackson knew the guys still had at least another thirty minutes on the road before getting back to Detroit.

Christian took it upon himself to serve Hunter with another vodka tonic. And Jackson rolled his eyes. He and Christian were not friends. They spent a few seconds in a stare down at the bar while Hunter nonchalantly sipped her last drink. She already had enough alcohol in her to not have a care in the world. Which was exactly how she wanted to feel right now. *Bash loved her, but she didn't know how to love him back. Aggie was going to die, but she wanted help with ending her life first.*

Jackson contemplated giving him a piece of his mind. They needed to leave, not be served more alcohol. He was so preoccupied with reminding himself to show self-restraint that he had not noticed when the door opened up and a few young adults, some of them likely underage, came through the door.

They were immediately carded, likely with fake ids, and then they split up. Two retreated to a corner booth and three more bolted toward the restrooms.

Christian asked Hunter something, but Jackson had not heard what he said. He did hear Hunter's response.

"Not tonight," she told him, and she looked serious, even sober, for that moment.

Christian not only looked forsaken, but he voiced his feelings a little too strongly. "What's his name? I heard about this new bodyguard," he glanced at Jackson, but knew he was her same ole driver who happened to be armed. Christian then glared at Hunter. "Have you kicked him out before dawn too?"

"That's enough!" Jackson chimed in.

"Jackson, it's okay," Hunter held up her hand to him. "It's time for us to go." What she should have answered was, *His name is Sebastian Perry and he loves me.* She just wished she was ready to feel deserving of his love.

Jackson stood up first, and Hunter followed. He was always surprised how steady she was on her feet, in high heels no less, when she had been drinking. She was never a boisterous, sloppy, falling-down drunk. She was a lady in the public eye who carried herself well in every circumstance.

"I have to pee before we leave," she whispered to Jackson, as Christian left them alone at the bar.

"Come right back," Jackson said, feeling no less impatient as he had all night. Getting her home safely was his only mission. Hunter giggled, and walked away from him. He looked at the door, and saw no one. He glanced around the restaurant at the crowd that was fairly quiet and had dwindled since they arrived. He then watched Hunter turn the corner for the ladies restroom.

Not even thirty seconds later, the door to Standby flew open, with Bash and Jay Marks rushing in. Jackson turned his head quickly. They were making an unnecessary scene, or so he had believed.

"Where is she?" Bash yelled to him, while still a good distance across the barroom from Jackson.

"Peeing," Jackson spoke up. And then he watched both Bash and Jay Marks rush down a small corridor that led to the restrooms. They had their guns drawn, and Jay Marks yelled back for Jackson to *" Watch the door because Jenkins' car was in the parking lot!"* Jackson felt his own face go pale.

Bash was the first to barge through the door of the ladies restroom. He called out her name as he stepped inside. "Hunter!" She was in there, in the last stall, pulling up her pants. She flung open the door and stuck her head out. "What the hell are you two doing?" Bash and Jay Marks exchanged quick glances. The relief on their faces was all consuming at the moment. Hunter stepped out, and zipped and buttoned her jeans in front of them, as Jay Marks walked over to the open window. "Was this window open when you came in here?"

Hunter looked up. "I don't know. I honestly never noticed."

"Were you alone in here before you went into the stall?" Bash asked her.

"As far as I know, yes. I never looked under the other stalls. I always use the last one. What is going on?"

"Jenkins' car is in the parking lot," Bash told her, and Jay Marks added, "I think he was in here, or maybe in the process of climbing through that window to get in here."

"Oh my God," Hunter responded. "I want to go home."

"It's about time," Bash threw his arm around her and escorted her out of that restroom.

"You drive her," Jay Marks spoke as he followed. "Jackson and I will stake out by our runaway's car for awhile."

That plan was foiled though when the El Camino was gone once they reached the parking lot just minutes later.

¥¥¥

Bash turned the deadbolt the moment they stepped inside of Hunter's home. "Thank you," she said.

"You already thanked me too many times on the drive here," Bash didn't want her gratitude. He only wanted her to realize how close she came tonight to truly getting hurt, or worse. All because she was acting fearless and out of control.

"I get the impression that you are miffed at me," Hunter called him out.

"I am so relieved that we got there in time," he told her. "But, yeah, you piss me off like no one else I've ever met in my entire life. You have to use your head. You are in serious danger right now, and your traipsing off to bars drinking and flirting like you don't have a care in the world."

"Flirting?" she asked him.

"Jackson kept us updated," Bash paused, because he hated how this felt, "and at one point he said he thought he would be driving both you and the bar owner, Christopher, back here."

"His name is Christian."

Whatever. "Are you involved with him?" Bash asked her outright. He didn't care if she lashed out at him for being too personal.

"I'm not involved with or committed to anyone," she told him, and Bash took her answer as an indication that she had slept with him before. He reminded himself that Hunter was going home alone tonight though. He hoped that meant he had some clout with her now. If not in her heart, then maybe he was at least on her mind.

"I've told you how I feel about you," Bash stated. "But I'm not going to pressure you. And I don't beg. I'm doing my job tonight and I'm staying here, but a guest room or the sofa will do."

"I want you to stay," she told him. They were again standing in the foyer, and she moved to the base of the stairs.

He didn't respond.

"Bash," she said his name and he felt his heart swell. "I'm so scared of so many things in my life right now. I'm going to lose the truest friend I've had for most of my life. I am being watched and hunted like an animal by another unstable human being. And," she paused, but forced herself to keep going, "I can't bring myself to choose to be happy with the man in front of me who says he loves me and he wants me, and that all I have to do is be ready and he'll be waiting."

Bash met her at the base of the stairway. "My heart breaks for you for so many reasons. I want you to heal, and more than anything I've wanted in a very long time — I wish you would take a chance on me. But, you're right, you have to be ready. I don't want to be someone who saves you. I think initially I believed that you needed to be saved. But now I see that what you need is someone to stand by your side as you save yourself."

Hunter forced the tears away. And she reached out to him with both of her hands. He took them in his. "Those might be the truest words you've spoken to me yet," she told him, and he was quick to shake his head.

"No. Well, maybe," he changed his mind and agreed with her, "but I told you something else earlier today that was the truth, too."

"That you're falling in love with me," Hunter closed her eyes for a moment. She wanted to say something more to him, but she refrained.

"I do love you," Bash responded, and he pulled her close. He held her with his strong arms wrapped around her, and Hunter held him back with all she had. And when she pulled away from him, she knew the time was finally right.

"Come upstairs with me. Stay with me tonight, Bash. I want to be with you."

He leaned into her, and she moved up on her tip toes. Their lips met, and this time they both knew there was no putting out this fire. No turning back. He followed her upstairs and into her bedroom.

"We've been this far before," he stated, "and you know that I'm going to ask if I'm staying with you until sunrise."

She nodded with teary eyes. "Please." Bash gathered her in his arms and kissed her full on the mouth. She wanted to feel his body, and be touched by him. They stood kissing and eagerly feeling for each other overtop their clothing. Hunter removed her shirt. Bash removed his. He helped her out of her jeans and heels. She stripped him of his denim and boots. They made their way over to her bed, and she climbed on top of him, straddling him through his underwear and hers. She took her off her bra, and he reached for her full breasts with both of his hands. He groaned when she freed his manhood into her own hands at the very same time. He touched her with two fingers between her legs. Those panties were in the way. He moved the lace aside and caressed her folds. She moaned. He lifted her entire body off of him and they removed their underwear together. He brought his mouth to her breasts, one and then the other. She arched her back in response. And he moved lower to find her core with his mouth. She cried out his name, and he nearly lost control. "I want you," he told her, as his mouth pleasured her again and again until she shuddered and finally collapsed with her release. "I want you more," she said aloud, her voice raspy, as he entered her. He lost his mind moving with her to find their rhythm. They rocked, touched, kissed, and each time he wanted to be deeper inside of her. And finally, he lost himself in her.

When he moved his body off of hers, Bash saw that she was crying. "Hunter? His first thought was that she regretted making love with him. "What's wrong?"

"Nothing. Nothing at all," she smiled, and her face was wet with tears. "For the first time, I am crying because *this* is happiness. I'm incredibly fulfilled by what you bring to my life. We made love. I never want to not feel like this. God, I need you." He wanted to kiss her again, but she stopped him. She had something else to tell him. "I love you, Bash."

Chapter 17

It wasn't quite sunrise, as it was too early, when Hunter sat up in her king-size bed and she wasn't alone. His dark hair was disheveled on his head, and she could see more overnight stubble growing on his chin and above his lip. He was a beautiful man, and so very good for her soul. She let the sheet fall from her upper body as she pulled her knees up to her bare chest. She thought of Aggie. Her trusted confidant, who she would want to, in just a matter of hours, tell all about the breakthrough she had last night. The peace she found. Her life already felt different. *She* felt different. This man beside her was a godsend for so many reasons. Aggie was going to be elated for her. She was one of those people who believed wholeheartedly in timing and everything happening for a reason. Hunter was comforted knowing that Aggie would be a part of this change in her life, as she knew that there would be so many moments ahead that she was going to face without her. Hunter made her a solemn promise yesterday. To be there. To help her. To guide her. And to hold her hand in her final moments of life. Aggie would decide when that time was to be. Hunter questioned how in the world she will be able to go through with what Aggie asked of her. But, for Aggie, she would.

She felt an open palm on her bare back. And then lips trailing her spine, upward, and consequently making her feel tingly all over. She turned her head and met her lips with his. "Good morning," he said to her with his mouth still on hers.

"It sure is," she giggled, as she wrapped her entire body around him. "I only have so much time…" she said, referring to having to be at the studio.

"I think we can make it work," he buried his face into her chest and savored a nipple with his tongue. She lowered herself on him then and aggressively straddled his hips as she completely bent forward. *The benefits of yoga.* She teased his manhood with her lips and then her tongue. He groaned. She guided herself overtop him all at once, until he was completely inside her. She moved over him slowly at first and then she accomplished her morning workout right there in her own bed. It was exhilarating for her to hear him call out her name. It was her turn to drive him to the brink. Last night, they made beautiful love for the first time. And, this morning, they had rough, mind-blowing sex.

¥¥¥

The time count was five…four…three…two…and one. "We're live," Hunter heard Bruce say in her ear monitor.

She stood solo in front of digital graphs, depicting the rise of student loan debt on the wall behind her. The camera angle gave way to a complete vertical length view of Hunter. She wore black skinny pants, three-inch black heels, and a short, double-breasted white jacket with gunmetal trim. Her white-blonde hair was down to her shoulders and styled with big, loose curls. She was again confident and prepared for today's scheduled story, which was initially supposed to air one day ago.

"As of 2018, more than forty-two million student loan borrowers have student loan debt of one hundred thousand dollars or less," she began. "More than two million student loan borrowers have student loan debt greater than one hundred thousand. And, four hundred and fifteen thousand of those two million have a debt greater than two hundred thousand. It's staggering. And, that means, roughly one in four American adults are paying off student loans. When they graduate, the average student loan borrower has thirty-seven thousand dollars in student loans, which is a twenty-thousand-dollar increase from thirteen years ago."

"In just a moment here, joining us at ABS will be several young adults who currently are either enrolled in college, or just beginning their search for one and they are all looking for ways to minimize their debt." The camera panned over to a round-table setting, where three young women and three young men were seated. They had laptops, backpacks, and stacks of paperwork with them to create a college-like feel. Hunter walked and spoke into the camera simultaneously. She now shared the same frame on camera with those students.

"Welcome everyone, this brings back some exciting ... and stressful... memories for me," she eyed them as a group and received smiles and laughter. Hunter didn't focus on any faces at the table, just yet, as she had a teleprompter to read, stating a few examples of how they could begin to minimize their debt. She had already individually met the six young adults yesterday at the studio. When the college debt story was postponed for one day, they were all given identification tags to return this morning. All six chairs at the round table were occupied. She began the segment by reading from the teleprompter that was feeding out her words directly below the camera. "We will get to know each of you individually as we progress here, because I want to know who's doing what to save money now and be debt-free when you obtain a college degree. It's important that you seek sources of free money, such as grants and scholarships — before turning to student loans. Depending on your specializations, I want to know who has committed to a less expensive college. What I am hoping all of you, who are watching, will walk away with from this experience here, is the knowledge to budget before you borrow." Hunter smiled as she completed conveying that information. She turned to her subjects then. She stood behind their table, in between a male and a female. The young woman had short, red, kinky-curly hair and freckles across the bridge of her nose. Hunter remembered her name as Suzie. She eyed the young man, opposite of Suzie, to test her memory of his name. He was wearing a Baker College hoodie, which she had briefly noticed earlier. Hunter looked down now, to get a better glimpse of his face as she began to speak. He looked up and directly at Hunter with an extremely unsettling expression on his face. His brown hair was stringy and his eyes were beady. Hunter immediately took two steps backward from being in close proximity to him.

Jimmy Jenkins.

He was there, and he was live on the air with them, and very much an unwelcomed part of the round table college debt story that Hunter completely lost sight of right now.

"Regroup," Bruce commanded in her ear. "You look like you've seen a ghost." There had already been entirely too many seconds of dead air, but Hunter wasn't able to recover or regain her composure. Not before Jimmy Jenkins spoke.

He abruptly stood up from the table, and kept his back to the cameras while he faced Hunter. "I finally caught up with you..."

Hunter shot her eyes past him and at the camera. "Cut to a commercial break," she stated, feeling as if she was in a trance. There was desperation in her eyes. Bruce stood straighter, and the hair on the back of his neck reacted. He instantly felt her panic, and knew that kid was not supposed to be on the set. He saw fear like that on Hunter's face once before. *When she was the victim of a stalker.*

"No! We stay live," Jimmy Jenkins turned to look past the cameras. "The cameras keep rolling or our star gets hurt!" He had no idea who he was barking this order at in that cluster of people standing off in the distance, but someone would listen. He was certain of it. But just to be clear, he added, "Get the rest of these people out of here! This so-called story isn't happening today." Hunter watched the young adults scurry off the set. They immediately looked to some of the nearby staff, off camera, for direction. The fact was, no one knew what the hell to do. *Run or hide?*

¥¥¥

Jay Marks had not checked the cameras at the estate all night long. He knew that Bash was there, with Hunter, and had kept her safe. He thought about the two of them, and hoped they would find a way to make their relationship work. His opinion was Bash was a good guy, and Hunter was deserving of happiness after all she had been through. But, most of all, he wanted Aggie to be at peace. Knowing Hunter had found love again would bring his dying wife that state of mind. He closed his eyes for a moment and remembered when she asked him to help her leave this world with dignity. He was afraid of what she might do in time to come, but he would not stop her. He had no right to expect her to suffer out of his own selfishness to prolong her time here, with him.

Bash walked through the basement door, and Jay Marks thought he heard him whistle.

"Are you whistling?" Jay Marks spun around in his swivel chair. "No one is that chipper this early in the morning unless they've gotten laid."

Bash laughed out loud.

Jay Marks waited.

"Okay, we were together last night. She wants me in her life. She loves me." Bash beamed and grinned from ear to ear.

"Well I'll be damn!" Jay Marks exclaimed. "Good for you, brother. I couldn't be happier for you both."

Bash nodded. Still smiling. "No need to review the cameras from last night. There was only activity in one room." They both laughed in unison like a couple of hormone-possessed boys in the locker room.

A second later, Bash looked around the room, on top of the desks and the main table. "Where are you hiding the TV remote? I want to watch the local news, Hunter should be live right now."

Jay Marks rolled his eyes, but smiled. *That man for sure had it bad.*

He found the remote control for the television mounted up on the wall. He powered it on, and flipped through a few channels to get to ABS 7. He stood in the middle of the room, looking up, and he froze the moment he saw what was happening. "What in the hell am I watching?"

Jay Marks turned to look.

Both of them stared.

"Is that Jenkins?" Jay Marks spoke aloud.

Bash pumped the volume high. "Oh my God. He's got her."

Chapter 18

Hunter drew in a slow deep breath through her nostrils. It was just her and that nineteen-year-old unstable kid on the set now. On live television. She was baffled why in the world he would demand for them to stay on the air.

"Hunter Raine, the television star," Jimmy Jenkins spoke to her in an obvious mocking tone. "It's just you and me now."

"And the entire viewing network," Hunter stated, wishing this would not be *making the news* right now. There certainly were other ways to get ratings. This, oddly, almost seemed like karma, considering all the things she had said or done over the years *to get the story*. Still, she didn't feel deserving of this insanity.

Bruce made certain that someone on staff immediately called 911. There were many crew members who scattered and sought help, leaving Jimmy Jenkins out-numbered as he clearly did not have this chaotic attempt under control. Both Bash and Jay Marks were among the emergency crew franticly on their way. Bruce was relieved to see Hunter handling this on her own right now. If she was panicked, she was still able to hold herself together enough to use her head. "Just talk to him and stall, the police are on their way," she heard Bruce in her ear monitor. His voice was strangely calm, and quieter. Hunter thought of the men on her security team. *Bash.* She could use some rescuing right about now. But she didn't want anyone to rush the scene and get hurt, or worse, trying to save her. First, she wanted to know what Jimmy Jenkins wanted, or what he had planned for her. There was no obvious weapon right now. And Hunter clearly wanted him to keep it that way.

"Let's get started," Jimmy Jenkins suggested and motioned toward the set where Hunter did a large portion of her interviews. There were just two chairs in place, where she was often one-on-one with her subject.

"Started with what?" Hunter asked him.

"My interview," he told her. "And I don't mean the college bullshit. It was a nice way for me to get in here unnoticed though." Hunter wondered what happened to the student who was supposed to be there today, the one whose temporary identity Jimmy Jenkins had stolen. *Were they friends? Or had he been hurt because he was in the way of this kid getting something that he wanted?*

"Go, come on. Sit!" Hunter eyed Bruce, past the cameras, and he simply nodded. She should do as he said. For now. The police were there, and in the corridors of the backstage.

Jenkins saw Hunter look at someone in the crew. He looked behind his back then. "If anyone tries anything, she will get hurt. No cops, you hear? This is my show with Hunter Raine, and I want my money's worth."

Hunter sat down in her typical anchor chair. Her knees were shaking, and she could feel the perspiration pooling between her breasts underneath her jacket. Jenkins sat directly across from her. "I will ask the questions," he demanded, and she only waited for him to continue.

"Let's tell America how you knew my brother," he spoke, and Hunter thought to herself, *he was a fucking stalker who murdered the man I was going to marry!* Hunter's persona on camera was vastly different, at times, than her real-life self. She seldom cared what other people, outside of her circle, thought. She didn't have to be prim and proper for anyone. If she wanted to curse, she cursed. If she wanted to drink, she drank. And most times she dressed seductively and went braless. She worked hard for the shapely body she had, and she was completely comfortable in her own skin. She had her own form of etiquette.

"Your brother," she began to think of what she was going to say as she spoke.

And backstage, Bash was going out of his mind. "We need to do something. His back is to us now, let's just take him out."

"On live television?" Jay Marks questioned his rationale. They were not even sure yet if he was armed, but assumed so.

"What is he even doing?" Bash felt helpless, and seriously confused by what was happening.

"Getting revenge," Jay Marks answered what they were all afraid to say.

"I think we all know that your brother had an obsession," Hunter spoke daringly, "with me."

Jimmy Jenkins responded, "He did, but you wouldn't give him the time of day. He used to cry because he cared about you so much. He would record your newscasts and watch them over and over. He used to tell me that you were going to be his wife someday. That's why he got rid of Aaron Cooper!"

Hunter stayed silent. She blinked her eyes a few times and clenched her jaw. Just hearing Cooper's name in that way made her cringe. Her heart would always hurt knowing that his life was taken, indirectly, because of her. She felt angry now. She stared at another Jenkins who was messing with her life. *Mentally unstable branches grew on that family tree.*

"My brother liked how you drink too much sometimes." Hunter probably should have felt embarrassed having that said on live television, but she wasn't. If anyone judged her now over Jenkins, they had the problem. "We should have a drink now, you know, to toast my brother's memory and all."

Hunter heard Bruce protest in her ear, "No."

And Bash and Jay Marks both came unglued backstage. "He'll drug her!" Bash spat at the law enforcement officers in their mix. "Let's just get this idiot now!"

Hunter was listening to her own pulse in her ears, when he spoke to her again.

"How about some choices," he stated, as he sat forward in his chair. There was a small coffee table separating them, and on it he emptied his pockets. Guns were already drawn and ready backstage. And there was a SWAT team sniper in the rafters above the clustered studio lights. His target was held steady on Jenkins' back.

He set down a small vile of white powder. And then he reached in the back of his jeans and retrieved a pistol. He also placed it on the table. "Which way would be best? A bullet or an overdose? I'm sure the reporter in you has some statistics filed in that smart brain of yours. Which one has the higher death rate? And, tell me, has this ever been done on live TV before?" He laughed boisterously, and Hunter nearly jumped out of her chair. Her emotions had run too high doing nothing these past however many minutes. She was done having him play this game with her life.

"So, you're going to take my life," Hunter boldly took a stand. She at least knew what his intentions were now. He had drugs, and a weapon, and one of them would kill her.

"I think that's only fair, considering that you took my brother from me. Even after that, your fans still adored you. I thought it would be a real eye-opener for them to see the end of you. Closure for everyone." Jenkins nodded his head repeatedly. Hunter could see the whites of his eyes were red, and one eye twitched profusely.

"What about for you?" Hunter asked him. "Your every move is digging you deeper into trouble right now. You could go to prison for the rest of your life."

He shrugged his shoulders. "Whatever. I don't have much to lose. This shirt on my back isn't even mine," he gestured toward the college hoodie he had stolen. Hunter thought she saw a glimpse of a genuine person. "I'll rest easy just knowing you are gone and I had everything to do with that." And then Hunter noticed the fear take over again when his words turned ugly.

Hunter was aware that this nineteen-year-old lived on his own, and had nothing to show for. No family. No money. No goals in his life. Just a crime record, and likely drugs in his system. Strangely, right now, she thought of the police deputy's widow she interviewed weeks ago. She was a woman who was trying to make a difference in lives like Jenkins'. She believed that there was a genuine person inside of each addict-turn-criminal that was worth reaching. And reforming.

Hunter was still terrified beyond reason right now. She carried a deep hatred for Ricky Jenkins for ruining her lifelong plans, and now for his little brother who was out of his mind with the intent to take her life. On television, no less. But, suddenly, those deeper thoughts that flooded her mind seemed to ease her fear.

"I know this isn't you, not really," she spoke to him. "We all live through things in our lives that threaten to turn us ugly, and into someone who we truly do not want to be. But it's just easier to put on that dishonest disguise to cover up the pain."

"Shut up. Okay! Just shut up. I'm calling the shots here. This is my show, not yours." Hunter believed she had gotten to him a little.

"I don't want to die," she told him, and gestured to the table where the gun and drug vile still were. "And you don't deserve to be locked up for the rest of your life."

"No choice," he blurted out. "There's no turning back now."

"I disagree," Hunter told him. "Walk away from this table with me. We can stop the cameras anytime."

"And then what?" he asked, while Hunter and everyone else watching them questioned if she really had gotten his attention, and that this could end peacefully. "Will you press charges?"

"Not if you check yourself into drug rehab."

"I think you are as crazy as I am," he spoke, and Hunter saw another glimpse of a teenage boy who seriously lost his way.

"Try me," she offered.

There wasn't even a moment's notice. In a split second, or less, Jimmy Jenkins grabbed for the pistol on the table between them with the intent to pull the trigger.

Hunter screamed.

The gun that he held mid-air was aimed at his own head when a bullet from the rafters instantly brought him down before he could fire.

Chapter 19

Both Bash and Jay Marks were holding onto her. Her feet were off the ground, as she was carried off the set, and away from a scene that ended in bloodshed. And, somehow, it had not been her own.

Suddenly Hunter felt as if she could not breathe. She gasped for air, and she felt as if she were going to choke, and then the tears broke free. Bash and Jay Marks set her down on the floor against the wall as soon as they reached the backstage area with her again. The police would handle Jenkins. The two men who were her personal security team, and who loved her, were relieved beyond belief to have her safe in their arms. They both knelt in front of her. That studio was swarming with emergency personnel and employees. They needed a quiet spot, away from the chaos. A safe corner on the floor was it right now.

"It's over. You're okay. Just get it out." Bash grabbed her around the shoulders and sat behind her, and Jay Marks kept rubbing her leg, and then he squeezed her hand and held it in his.

"You were amazing out there," Jay Marks told her, and she shook her head no.

"Yes, you were," Bash continued. "I think being a badass reporter saved your life. There were times when we all had to remind ourselves that we weren't watching an interview, because you were so composed." Bash may have embellished that truth because he personally had been focused and frantic the entire time, but he meant well. "You kept calm, and you got to him. You saved your own life, Hunter."

"Who shot him?" Hunter calmed herself enough to speak."

"SWAT in the rafters," Jay Marks told her.

Hunter shook her head, "How awful." Neither of them understood exactly what she meant by that. *Awful that he was shot? Awful, as in this whole experience for her?* "He was going to kill himself," she added, as if no one else witnessed what she did.

"The threat to your life was made," Bash began. "There was no question that when he picked up the gun, shots were going to be fired at him, even if everyone saw him aim at himself."

"Did they kill him?" Hunter wanted to know.

"Don't know," Bash said, but he certainly hoped he was dead. *Locking away that unstable kid was not going to be enough.* Bash's life, that he hoped for with Hunter, flashed before his eyes today. *He could have lost her.*

"We will know more later," Jay Marks told her. "Right now, let's get you off the floor and out of here."

"Not yet," she heard a voice at her feet, and she looked up to see Bruce. She jumped up and fell into his arms. His face was wet with tears, and she held onto him for dear life.

"Your voice in my ear monitor calmed me," she told him, and he shook his head as if the compliment was untrue.

"Nonsense. I could not have felt more helpless, or useless to you. Thank goodness you were unharmed. I am so sorry he got in here. Whoever he got past will be fired."

"No," Hunter said. "Please don't."

Bruce took both of her hands in his own. "I think it's finally time for me to start thinking about retirement. I've been behind the camera for it all now." They laughed a little together, and Hunter could see that there was some truth to his words.

"I, I, I c-c-could use some ll-love, too." Hunter turned around quickly toward that voice. The stutter broke her heart. Aggie opened her arms and Hunter lunged toward her, but she immediately held her back with some resistance as Aggie had felt somewhat fragile to her. "You," Aggie stopped trying to speak and attempted to swallow, but she appeared to have difficulty. Her husband immediately went to fetch some water for her. "You are so, so ver-ry ll-lucky to be here."

Hunter wholeheartedly agreed with her, "I know."

¥¥¥

The last thing she wanted to do was go home midday and rehash everything that happened repetitively in her mind. Hunter opted to show up at the emergency staff meeting that Bruce had called. They were going to discuss, in Hunter's absence, how their network would handle this story. Because it was a story. It was news that the entire City of Detroit was talking about. And, while all of the competing news channels were recapping the story, ABS 7 needed to approach it in a different, more sensitive manner, out of respect for one of their own.

Bruce was dictating precisely that when Hunter walked into the conference room. He immediately stood up. "I thought you went home," he spoke as if she were a fragile child.

"No," she answered in front of everyone. "I've been in my office, thinking, and I came to the conclusion that since this is about me, because the viewers saw it happen to me, I need to be the one to go back on the air and talk to them. I was thinking tomorrow morning, if that's okay with all of you," she looked around the conference room, "because then we will know more about *his* condition." All everyone knew as of now was that Jimmy Jenkins was alive. He was still breathing when he was taken to the emergency room at Henry Ford Hospital. Bash and Jay Marks were there and waiting to follow up on his condition.

Bruce offered Hunter the chair beside him. She sat down, as he addressed her with more compassion on his mind than business. "You don't have to do this, if it's too much, too soon. You are a true professional though. Not many journalists would be ready to jump right back in."

"My work is why I need to be back on the air," she began. "I don't want to fear being in front of the camera. That's not who I am."

One of the female executives at the table who was at least a decade older than Hunter chimed in, "That a girl! Don't let him win."

Hunter smiled, but kept silent. This wasn't at all about a troubled teenager taking anything away from her. She had not felt less whole after the crazy encounter on the news set today. In fact, a new understanding had enveloped her thoughts. She had a chance to make a difference. She could use her position in the public eye to do it. And that was why she wanted to be a part of this staff meeting. She wanted to share her vision and see how well-received it would be.

¥¥¥

Hunter was in her living room with only one thing on her mind. Work. She sat bent forward on her ivory sofa with a laptop and several files of printed paperwork scattered all over the glass-top coffee table. She had been lost in her research and had no concept of how much time has passed. A text from Bash, that he was entering the gate, interrupted her. She jumped up to unlock the deadbolt on the front door and immediately sat back down again. She replied to his text in the process. *Door's open.*

When Bash opened the door himself and came in, he looked puzzled. "This is a first," he said, pointing at the door. "You're keeping it unlocked now?"

Hunter briefly glanced up at him and then back at her laptop. Her hair was pulled up high on her head in a sprout-like ponytail, and she wore glasses tonight. The amount of reading she had to do was already straining her eyes, so she had taken out her contacts. She also had changed into lounge clothes for total comfort while she worked. A white tank top and her favorite loose white yoga pants. "No. It's been locked. I just got up now, so you could come right in."

Bash could tell she was preoccupied. Or downright busy. He wondered if that was how she coped with anything traumatic. She just threw herself into her work. He walked over and didn't hesitate to sit down on the sofa beside her. He didn't need to wait for an invitation. The two of them were way past that stage in their relationship. He noticed she had a glass of wine on the table. It was almost completely full, but a lipstick stain on the rim exposed that she had sipped it.

"I have the latest on Jenkins' condition," Bash spoke cautiously, and he immediately had her attention.

She turned, and he watched her lift her glasses off her nose. He thought she looked both business-like and sexy with specs. *And just plain sexy without a bra again.* "How is he?" Hunter knew that he had survived the gunshot wound to his back, but that was all.

"He'll live," Bash began. "He's actually a very lucky son of a bitch, as the bullet did not come into contact with his spinal cord or any major organs or nerve roots. The damage was minor as the bullet apparently turned once it entered the body, and then it deflected off of a bone before exiting out the side of his body." Hunter listened raptly and imagined the entire process.

"So he just has some healing to do?" Hunter asked.

"Pretty much. The doctor described the initial bullet wound and the exit wound as bad cuts." Hunter nodded her head. Bash watched her for a moment before he asked what she was thinking.

"I'm not sure," she answered honestly. "I guess I didn't want him to be seriously hurt, or worse."

"It would be completely understandable if you did!" Bash had wished him dead. He never wanted that poor excuse for a human being to have the opportunity to get that close to Hunter ever again. Bash watched Hunter reposition her glasses on her nose and turn to her work again. He wondered if he shouldn't push too hard. She appeared to have subconsciously blocked out, or purposely forced out of her mind, what happened this morning. "What are you working on?" he asked, partly wishing he had found just her and her wine glass when he walked in. Like he had a few times before. He was hoping to have dinner with her, and to comfort her in his arms. He had expected her to be upset. But a few of their exchanged texts today had also been unemotional on her end.

She turned to Bash again, and seemed interested in sharing something with him. "I'm going back on the air tomorrow morning." Bash nodded. He truly wasn't all that surprised, considering her current mood tonight. She was all business.

"I think that's okay, if it's something you believe you're ready for."

"I am." Hunter was confident. "I have an idea for something, and I really do think I am going to just run with it. I would like for you to be the first person, outside of the studio, that I share it with." Bash felt flattered. This was the first time since he walked in the door tonight that he felt like she wanted him to be there. That they were close like a couple. He chided himself for needing that reassurance, or the attention, because Hunter had been through insanity today and she was the one who deserved his reassurance and attention.

"I definitely want to hear it then." Bash reached for her and gently rubbed her back. It was the first time they had touched since he arrived. She seemed unaffected by his physical contact. He took his hand away then.

"I was really scared today." *Finally, she wanted to talk about it,* Bash thought to himself, and listened. "All I could see when I looked at him was this crazed person who wanted to hurt me. And then, I don't know what it was or what was said or done to make me see through his evil and unstable persona, but I did. I saw a helpless kid who chose violence to conceal his pain. Grief drove him to that place."

Bash was silent. This wasn't Hunter Raine. Life had hardened her and toughened her. And he had actually liked that about her. She was strong and, well, she didn't take anything from anyone. This reaction was entirely different.

"You said so yourself, that I got to him," Hunter reminded him, "that I saved my own life. I do believe I reached him in that last desperate moment."

Bash was confused. "He was going to shoot himself." As if Hunter needed to be reminded of that.

"But initially it was me that he was going to take out. He didn't want to hurt me after all, I guess. He just wanted to end his life. I would like to believe that he felt remorseful."

"He's crazy, Hunter." Bash was irritated, but he tried to focus. "What does this have to do with your story idea?"

"I had an epiphany. I truly did. And now I feel obligated to help people like Jenkins who are struggling with something that's bringing them down to places where they don't want to be. Those who are turning to drugs and crime can be helped. Some can be reached before they fall into any of that."

"I don't really follow where you are going with this," Bash admitted.

"I want to open a safehouse, so to speak, right here in Detroit. It's not going to be secretive or on the down low. This place will be a public building for people to go to when they need help, and have nowhere else to turn. I want to help people in Cooper's memory. I thought about calling it, The Coop."

Bash ran his fingers through his dark hair. "You can't singlehandedly change the world, sweetheart. It's just not that simple."

"But I can do this. I want to use my very public position to reach people. There will be free counseling, food, showers, clean clothing, and a place to stay until these people can get back on their feet." The Coop would also be a shelter. Not so much for the homeless, but geared toward people teetering on the edge from addiction, or whatever plagues them.

Bash shook his head. "It's too dangerous. You're a local celebrity and this idea of yours could attract more unstable admirers."

"It's not like I will be working there, Bash. It's just something I want to spearhead. You know, to make a difference."

"Sounds as if your mind is already made up," Bash nearly scoffed. "You wanted my opinion and I gave it to you. It's a bad idea all around."

Now Hunter was unnerved. "No, I wanted you to hear my idea. I never asked for your opinion. I welcome it, I do, but I disagree with you."

Bash softened for a moment. "I just want to keep you safe, that's all." He was tempted to add, *and you have to be smart about this,* but he refrained.

"I know," she said, and she reached for his hand. He held hers back. "I really have a lot of work to do before I meet with Bruce again first thing in the morning." She never turned back toward her laptop or any of the papers scattered on that table. But Bash could see that's where her focus was. Her mind was not on them tonight. She didn't need his comfort, or his opinion that was only meant to protect her from harm's way.

"I'll go," he said. And before he stood, he leaned into her and pressed his lips to her forehead. "Call you tomorrow," was all he said before he got up and walked out the door. Bash stood on that massive front porch for a long moment, and he waited to hear Hunter turn the deadbolt on the other side of the door. But she never did.

Chapter 20

"She's not dealing with this in a healthy way," Bash expressed to Jay Marks the following day as they sat vigil in front of the camera feed from Hunter's estate. She was already at the studio, preparing for her return on the air, just twenty-four hours after all of Detroit viewed her encounter with a crazed and unstable young man.

"I've known Hunter for a long time, and my wife has known her the longest," Jay Marks spoke. "She's like no one else I've ever met. Certainly not like other women, but I think you already should know that. She puts herself out there in some ways and doesn't think twice, and yet she also knows how to close off her own emotions from herself. It's like she's able to keep her mind and her heart from being in sync sometimes, as a way to avoid the pain. And not have to face the effects of a traumatic experience."

"I understand all of what you're explaining," Bash stated, "but I still don't know what to do about it. I feel like her rash decisions will only end up hurting her."

"You can't stop her," Jay Marks spoke as if he had long accepted that fact.

"It's not that I want to control her decision-making," Bash defended himself. "I respect and admire her independence and the fierce way that she's her own support system. She doesn't need anyone else to be in her corner."

"That's not entirely true," Jay Marks responded. "She needs people. She just picks and chooses very carefully who those people are going to be. Look around. There's Aggie. There's Bruce. I count myself and her entire security team in that. She needs her viewers or her fans, too. She can't do what she does and be successful without them. And then there's you."

Bash stayed silent.

"I didn't think she would do it. She opened up her heart to you. That says something. You're special to her. So don't mess that up." Jay Marks looked away for a moment, as there were landscapers on the grounds of the estate.

Bash again caught his attention. "So then what do I do?"

"You love her, but leave her wild."

"That sounds both intoxicating and exhausting."

They both laughed.

"That's love sometimes," Jay Marks shook his head.

"You really do trust that she will be okay, don't you?" Bash asked him, referring to everything that Hunter sinks herself into.

"I do," he said. "I will share something with you that I have not told anyone, and don't plan to. Ever. The boys and I are going to lose Aggie. The dynamics of ALS is nothing but pure devastation. My wife confided in me that she wants to die with dignity." Bash realized that meant only one thing. Aggie did not want to allow ALS to progress and wreak havoc on her body and soul. He could see the tears welling up in Jay Marks' eyes as he spoke of what lied ahead. "She asked me to help her. But, I can't. I can't live with that."

Bash sat there, watching a big, burly man slowing breaking.

"I told her to turn to Hunter."

Both men sat there and shared silence.

¥¥¥

"And we're live..." Hunter heard Bruce in her ear monitor. She was back on the air. Back in the saddle, so to speak. It's what people said when someone returned to something, often times after a set-back. But Hunter hadn't given herself time to wait, or waste. Those closest to her didn't believe that to be a good thing. But she clearly chose to do everything her own way.

On camera, Hunter sat, legs crossed, and perched on a single stool in the forefront of the set where the shooting took place the day before. She wore a deep burgundy silk button-down blouse with an oversized collar, and flared, wide-legged black dress pants with matching pointed-toed heels. Her hair was in an updo, showing the vast contrast between her dark roots and white blonde highlights. There were large silver hoops dangling from her ears. She looked striking. Even her eyes were bright and youthful. She did not look at all like a woman who had been through what she just endured live on air.

"Good morning, Detroit," she began, without a teleprompter, at her own request. "I'm Hunter Raine. I believe many of you may be surprised to see my return this morning, so soon after what took place right here in our ABS NewsChannel 7 studio yesterday. Someone backstage complimented me very sincerely this morning, because they were proud of me for facing my fears. While I appreciate that notion, I do not fear this spot right here. This studio is home for me. These people behind the camera, directing me, and speaking in my ear," she briefly touched her earpiece, "are my strength, and my family. And you, my viewers out there, I'm very much aware of the outpouring of support and love. I've read your emails to the studio and I've read your posts on social media. Thank you all." Hunter smiled at the camera, paused, and then began again.

"I will not have an on-air guest today during my segment. I am going to do something out of the norm instead. I'd like to share with you, first, an update on the medical condition of the young man whose name was released by the authorities after he initially threatened my life, and then made a dire attempt to take his own life, before he was gunned down by law enforcement." Hunter took a moment to inhale a breath through her nostrils. *Did she really just say that?* It still all seemed unreal to her.

"Jimmy Jenkins was hospitalized and treated for minor damage from a bullet wound," Hunter remembered, verbatim, what Bash had told her. "Fortunately, the bullet did not come into contact with his spinal cord or any major organs or nerve roots. The damage was reported as minor because the bullet apparently turned once it entered the body, and then it deflected off of a bone before exiting out the side of his body."

"The victim is going to survive," Hunter spoke, "but what is ironic —and you are all likely thinking the same thing as you're watching right now— is he wasn't the victim of yesterday's events. I was. Or, at least, I was intended to be. I'm grateful to be unharmed. But, something did happen to me on this set yesterday. Something entirely unexpected. And I would like to share that with all of you." Hunter carried on, completely composed, and she also refrained from mentioning what will come of Jimmy Jenkins' fate. It was public knowledge that he would face criminal charges, but Hunter was not prepared to mention that. In any case, this was an up close and personal look at Hunter Raine today. Just weeks ago, she shared her private pain of grief. Her own personal story of struggle. And now, she was becoming even more real to the viewers.

"Until yesterday, I don't think it ever occurred to me to consider that there really is a genuine person inside of each addict-turned-criminal that is worth reaching. And reforming. I simply associated people who do terrible things to be terrible people," she stated. And it was a bold statement. "I believe now that I was wrong. On air, I made an attempt to reach that young man yesterday. If you were watching, I told him that we all live through things in our lives that threaten to turn us ugly, and into someone who we truly do not want to be. And, sometimes, it's just easier to put on that dishonest disguise, because then we can also cover up the pain. I honestly believe that's true. And I want to help."

"Imagine a place in our City of Detroit that has the purpose of a safehouse and a shelter all in one. It will not be a place that is discreet or disclosed. This will be a public building for anyone who is struggling, to seek help in the form of free counseling. It will also provide food and a temporary place to stay. I do not want to singlehandedly change the world,"

Hunter thought of Bash's words. "My only hope is to spearhead a project to reach people in their time of need."

"And finally, my hope is to name this building, The Coop, after my love who I lost too soon. He was an integral part of our crew here at ABS NewsChannel 7 and he will always hold a special place in my heart. And I can't think of a better way to honor him." Hunter smiled into the camera.

"Fifteen seconds…" she heard Bruce in her ear monitor.

"I'll leave you to ponder this idea of mine that I hope to bring to life. I do welcome your comments or questions about The Coop, which I will address and answer live on air tomorrow morning. Thank you all for watching. I'm Hunter Raine. ABS NewsChannel 7."

"And that's a wrap. Proud of you, girl." Off the air, Hunter smiled past the cameras as she caught Bruce eyeing her with that pleased expression on his face which she never let herself take for granted.

Chapter 21

She felt good about herself. This was different than reporting a feel-good story to tug at the heartstrings of her viewers. This felt like her baby, an idea she wanted to give life to.

Hours later, Hunter had returned to the studio with her camera crew, after pre-taping portions of a story that would air tomorrow morning. She sat down at her desk in her private office, just as her cell phone rang.

She answered on the second ring, and smiled as she had seen the caller identification. "Well hello," she said into the phone, still relishing the feelings harbored in the beginning stages of falling in love.

"Two things," Bash said, and his voice warmed her. "One — you looked beautiful on camera this morning."

"That's all I get? Only beautiful?" she teased. "Why not hot or sexy or something entirely inappropriate?"

"I'll save that for later..."

Hunter giggled on her end.

"What's the second thing? You said there were two..."

"I'm picking you up today, not Jackson. You and I have plans."

"We do?" Hunter was unaware, but she certainly didn't mind the idea of spending time with Bash. She felt guilty for rushing him off last night while she was distracted by her work. Too long after he had left, she finally sat back on the sofa and wished he had stayed there with her.

"Absolutely," she heard him say. "I thought we'd take a drive around the city and scope out the available real estate. I've done some research online for you, and there are a few vacant buildings that I'd like to show you. Who knows? One might be perfect for your future plans."

Hunter paused on the opposite end of the phone. He was thinking of her, and he wanted to help her with this brand-new idea that she wanted so badly to see come to life. He supported her.

She finally responded. "You want to help me find a place for The Coop?"

"I do," he replied. "I assumed you have not had the time to think about possible locations."

"I haven't yet, no," she stated. "Thank you, Bash. This means so much to me. I don't think you realize how much. I'm the kind of girl who is used to getting things done on her own. I'm so touched that you want to help me." His willingness to support her also caught her off guard.

"Not only do I want to help, but I'd like to take you out to dinner, or back to your house with take-out, after our driving around mission is compete. Completely up to you." Bash had taken Jay Marks' advice. He was going to be there for Hunter, no matter what she was up to next.

"Only if you'll stay with me tonight?"

"You don't have to ask me twice." She was worth the trouble, Bash didn't need to convince himself. The stress and anxiety he had about protecting her, and keeping up with her sudden whims was well worth loving her.

"Bash," she said, and he felt his entire body tighten. "About last night… you were gone before I realized I was consumed with my research, and had not given you much attention. I know you were there to check on me because you care."

"I do care," Bash told her, "and I also love."

She giggled at his phrasing.

"Pick me up in one hour, my love."

On opposites ends of the phone, they both beamed. This was happiness.

¥¥¥

Bash chose where they were going to have dinner. Capers was a casual bar and restaurant on Gratiot Avenue, not too far from Standby, which was always Hunter's pick, especially for the bar. The two of them were sitting at a booth, because he insisted booths were more private.

"Have you been here before?" he asked her, and she nodded as she sipped what that bar was noted for — a swimming pool-size cocktail. Hunter was drinking what was called giggle juice, which was a combination of Moscato and vodka.

"I have. The steak by the ounce is hugely popular here in Detroit."

Bash grinned at her. "You're hugely popular here in Detroit." She giggled, but it wasn't the drink. It was the company.

"Thank you for driving me around. There are definitely some possibilities to look into," she noted again, as she had when they were in Bash's car and she was snapping photos with her cell phone from the side of the street.

"But nothing feels like the place, yet," he stated, and understood.

"Right," she sipped her giggle juice through the long straw and realized it was going down faster that way. She would for sure need another one before they ordered dinner. "I want an existing building. I want a good location, but not smack in the middle of downtown, or too far out of the city limits."

Bash took a generous sip of the beer on tap that he ordered. "Something will turn up. You have plenty of time. No one expects you to slap this plan together tomorrow."

"I know," Hunter agreed, "but I'm just anxious to see it happen." Bash was going to reach for her hand across the table, but they were interrupted by two men, who clearly were a couple.

"Hunter Raine, oh my gosh!" One of the guys with a pretty face and the overuse of product in his blonde hair spoke first. "We adore you! We watch you on ABS every single day."

"Thank you," Hunter smiled, and then glanced at Bash, hoping he understood that this happened to her in public sometimes. These two were harmless, she could tell.

"Could we get a photo with you?" the opposite guy spoke this time. His dark brown locks were pulled back into a man bun.

Hunter slid out of the booth, and stood between the two of them. The guy with product in his hair handed Bash his phone. "Do you mind?" Bash obliged.

When the two men left, one of them squealed as they walked away, and Hunter laughed at out loud. "Sorry," she looked at Bash after she was seated across from him in the booth again.

He held up his hand. "No big deal." *Just as long as you're safe,* he thought to himself. Tonight, he carried a handgun in the holster concealed underneath his shirt.

"What are you having to eat?" she opened the menu on the table.

"New York Strip."

"Filet for me," Hunter decided, "and I have to get the cheesy French onion soup!"

"Baked potato for me," Bash laughed as he chose the healthier option. Hunter's body certainly didn't look like she ever splurged on anything cheesy.

"You can try mine," she winked at him. And for a moment, they both took it in. This was something so trivial, but sharing food and being entirely comfortable in each other's presence was something they both had missed in their lives after they separately lost their loves.

"What are you thinking about?" he asked her, as her straw made a slurping sound at the bottom of her empty fish bowl glass.

"Two things," she responded. "I need another drink… and it looks like I have a lady fan headed my way. She keeps staring at me, well, at both of us."

Bash turned his head and instantly recognized the woman.

"Hi," she said to Bash, first, as she reached their booth. Hunter raised an eyebrow. She had misinterpreted the stares. This woman wanted to approach Bash, not her.

"Hello, Phyllis. How are you?" Bash stood, and gave the woman a friendly, close hug. And when he stepped away from her, he sat down again as she spoke.

"I'm good. How are you, Bash?" she asked before she made direct eye contact with Hunter. She was a curvy-built woman with shoulder-length red hair, and freckles across the bridge of her nose.

"I'm well. This is Hunter—"

"Hunter Raine, ABS news," the woman spoke with a soft smile. "I heard the two of you were seeing each other." At that moment, Hunter's suspicion that this woman was a former lover was practically confirmed. She wore a jealous, disapproving look.

"Allow me to explain to Hunter, who you are," Bash looked away from Phyllis and then back at Hunter. "Hunter, this is Phyllis. She is my late wife's sister."

Hunter tried not to let her face fall. She was entirely wrong with her initial assumption. She offered her hand to Bash's former sister-in-law. "It's nice to meet you."

"You too," Phyllis responded, but she didn't appear genuine. She wasn't starstruck like the two gentlemen who visited their table prior. She was far from even liking Hunter at the moment. In her eyes, Hunter understood, as she was in her sister's place. Despite the fact that her sister was gone.

"How are Dave and the kids?" Bash interjected.

"Doing well, thanks."

"I'm overdo for an Uncle Bash visit," he chuckled a little, and eyed his beer as if he wanted to take a long gulp of it.

"Yes, you are. Stop by anytime," Phyllis said, and she started to back away. "You too, Hunter. I suppose I just need to get used to seeing Bash moving on." Hunter nodded, but kept silent. She didn't know the last time she felt so uncomfortable.

Bash spoke first once she left their table. "Why did that have to be so awkward?" Bash kept his voice low, and then finally tipped his glass of beer to his mouth.

Hunter waved a hand in front of her face. She wished her drink glass was not empty at the moment. "It's fine. If I had a sister, I would completely get that." Suddenly, Hunter felt a wave of sadness. Aggie was like a sister to her. And when the day comes, however far down the road that may be, Jay Marks may fall in love with someone else. She imagined Phyllis' behavior to be mild compared to her own. *Someday.*

Bash noticed she was lost in thought when their waiter interrupted them to bring Hunter another drink, and to take their dinner order.

"Tell me about her," Hunter said to Bash when they were alone again.

"Phyllis? Or my late wife?"

"What was her name?" Hunter asked, feeling compassionate because they shared the same pain from losing their great loves.

"Kathryn," he told her.

"Did she look like her sister?"

"No, not really. Her hair was brown, sandy-brown, was what she used to call it. No freckles. She was taller, and thinner, and younger than Phyllis. She was a pediatric nurse."

"And you miss her," Hunter stated, and Bash was amazed by her willingness to talk about this. They hadn't shared anything like this with each other yet. "She was your wife. You were making a life with her, and all of it was ripped away from you both. I get that, Bash. No need to feel awkward with me. You've been so understanding, driving me around town this evening, as I go on and on about the building I'm going to name after Cooper. I want to be as understanding with you."

This time he reached for her hand across the table, and held it. "You really are something," he said. "Our losses have bonded us. I like who we are together. And I also like who we've been before, if that makes any sense at all." Bash shrugged.

"Perfect sense," Hunter agreed. "All of the people in our lives form us. I don't want to forget my time with Cooper, just like I don't expect you to disregard your life with Kathryn." Hunter paused before she added, "I like who we are together, too."

Chapter 22

He kissed her the moment they were in his car, just outside of the restaurant. She deepened that kiss and asked him to take her home. *Quickly.*

They moved respectively past the cameras downstairs, on the stairway, and in the hallway leading to Hunter's bedroom. The moment they closed the door, they were in each other's arms. She seductively backed her body up against the closed bedroom door. Bash held her hands high above her head and pressed his body into hers. He kissed her hard and full on the mouth. She responded. He released her hands in the air and began to unbutton the deep burgundy blouse she had worn live on television this morning. She had never changed out of those clothes tonight, as Bash had picked her up at the studio. He eyed her black bra, and her full breasts underneath the lace. He touched her, while she ran her fingers through his thick, dark hair. She put her hands underneath his t-shirt and immediately felt his gun. He backed away and took off the holster, and set it and the gun on one of Hunter's dresser tops nearby. She had two in that immense bedroom. He untied and kicked off his boots and socks. He stood in front of her barefoot in jeans. Hunter ran her hands over his fit chest. He pulled her into a kiss again, while he reached behind her with one hand and unclasped her bra. He touched her free, bare breasts, with his hands first, and then met them, slowly, one at a time, with his mouth. He was practically on his knees in front of her, bending down to her chest. Her black flared pants fell to her ankles, at her doing. Her thong, also black and lacy, drove him wild. "Sexy. Beautiful. I want you," he spoke all in one.

"Then take me," she said to him, as she reached for the button and zipper on his denim. She wiggled him out of those, and the bulge behind his boxer-briefs now drove her past the point of temptation. She touched him through the dry-fit material, and then got those off and out of the way too. Bash rolled his eyes back in his head when she touched him, there, with both of her hands. Open palms. And fingers. He dropped to his knees in front of her and moved her panties off with his teeth. He found her core as she stood with her back pressed up against the bedroom door. Her knees were weakening as she gripped his broad, bare shoulders. She dug her fingernails into him when he brought her breathless and to the brink of insanity. She released. She shuddered. And Bash picked her up and carried her naked body over to the bed. She kissed him hard and full on the mouth as he entered her. "I want to feel like this forever," he heard her say to him. He moved further inside of her, and rocked over her. Looking at her. Touching her. Caressing every inch of her body. And then he found his release with the woman he now loved more than anything.

¥¥¥

They laid spent in each other's arms. Hunter had one of her legs draped over his middle, with her head on his bare chest.

"I never thought that I would feel like this again," she told him in her dark bedroom where the only sound was their breathing and the soft whisper of her voice right now.

"Oh I knew," he responded with total confidence, as he traced her jawline with one finger. "For myself, I mean. The moment I saw you, I knew."

She giggled. "Men crush on me. I'm on TV." She rolled her eyes at herself. "I'm not going to lie. I was seriously attracted to you," she lightly kissed him on the lips, before she continued, "but beyond getting you into my bed, I did not imagine it to be like this for me again."

"I love when you talk like that. About me. About us."

"Us. We are an us," Hunter repeated.

"Always," Bash told her and then he pulled her close and kissed her.

"Promise?" she asked him, with her lips still on his.

"Yes. I promise you. We are going to be like this forever."

Believing that to be true came so effortlessly for the two of them, despite their losses and full understanding of how life could be suddenly and painfully unexpected.

¥¥¥

Jay Marks knew where they were. He wasn't going to disrupt their time together with a phone call to either of them. It was midnight, and time for him to sign out. He was going home to his wife. They had plans to go away for the weekend, as a family of four. There was an indoor water park that Aggie was anxious for the boys to experience. The strength and the balance in her legs had been failing her lately, more so than ever. She pressed for this trip, now, as she wanted to still be able to make memories with the boys. She was determined to swim and frolic in the water with them. *Remember to take lots of pictures…*

On Saturday morning, Bash read an email from Jay Marks. Hunter was in the kitchen, wearing only the t-shirt that Bash had worn the night before. He walked in, shirtless in his denim.

"There's my shirt," he wagged a finger at her. She turned around from the stovetop, and giggled.

"Want it back?" she teased him.

Bash chuckled under his breath. "Being served breakfast by a naked woman is awfully tempting…"

She threw her head back and laughed as she turned back around to the stove to scramble some eggs.

Bash held his phone as he sat down at the island. "I got an email from Jay last night. I guess he didn't want to call or text, as we were busy…" Hunter turned around from the stovetop, and listened. It didn't bother her in the least to know that Jay Marks was aware they were sleeping together. "He's taking Aggie and the kids to Great Wolf Lodge this weekend."

"In Traverse City?" It was a four-hour drive from Detroit.

Bash confirmed that with a nod.

"Oh, I didn't know that," Hunter stated, pushing the lever down on the toaster. She paused and thought for a moment how Aggie now had a bucket list of all the things she wanted to do and see, especially with her children, before—

Hunter stopped short her own train of thought. "Did he say how Aggie was feeling? She's been vague when I've asked her, and to be honest I haven't asked her lately. I think, sometimes, that if I don't acknowledge it, it will go away." Hunter turned her back to Bash, and switched off the stove burner. When the toast was ready, they would eat the eggs she had scrambled. Bash got up and walked to her. He extended his arms, and she fell into them.

"I'm here for you," she heard him say. And he was thinking how Hunter would never break the confidence of her best friend. Nor would he ask that of her. But, knowing what Jay Marks had said, Bash questioned if Hunter would ever confide in him if the time comes and Aggie depended on her to go through with it.

"I'm not going to know how to live without her, someday, you know," she admitted. Bash let her go, and helped her with breakfast. He buttered the toast while she scooped the eggs on two plates. And then, when they sat down together, to eat, he responded to what she said.

"I'm not going to tell you that you're strong, and you will be okay. We both know, from experience, how tiresome that is to hear. People are not strong because they were made that way. Strength is obtained when you are forced to put one foot in front of the other in order to survive."

Hunter wholeheartedly believed that. "I need to spend some time with her. Real, quality time. I've thought about asking Bruce for a leave of absence…when the time comes, one day." Bash noticed how she kept referring to the last days of Aggie's life as far off in the distance, possibly not even foreseeable or reachable. *One day. Someday.*

"What's going to happen to her? What is this illness capable of?" Bash asked, not knowing the specifics of ALS. He was unfamiliar with the disease, but he was aware of people ending up wheelchair-bound and without any ability to communicate.

"It attacks the nerve cells," Hunter began, as if she had done her research. Or maybe, she was just well educated in everything, as Bash believed. "And eventually, it renders a person disabled before killing them. Any way you decipher it, it's fatal." Bash could hear the anger and bitterness in her voice. She pushed her breakfast plate aside.

"I'm sorry. I'm being insensitive. I wondered if you wanted to talk about it, that's all, and Jay's email started these thoughts for me."

"It's alright," Hunter reassured him. "I guess I'm still in denial. She's my best friend. I would do absolutely anything for her."

"I know," Bash stated, and he did know the lengths she would go. And he also was certain Hunter was not going to confide in him about this. Not now. Maybe not ever. Euthanasia, or mercy killing, was illegal. And it was a black or white topic that divided people. *In favor of it. Against it. Would never do it. Absolutely would do it to end someone's suffering.* Somehow, Bash believed that Hunter likely never had a strong opinion about it before now. What it had come down to for her, however, was she supported her best friend. No matter what.

Chapter 23

On Monday morning, Hunter was at the studio and in the hair chair. She wasn't at all accustomed to waiting on Aggie — it was always the other way around — but that's what she was doing now. Ernie, from makeup, walked into the room. Hunter looked at him through the mirror. "What's going on?" she asked, as he had already painted her face to look and feel beautiful for television.

"Let's just straighten your hair today," he stated, with a glum look on his face. "I can do it. I'm good at it. Or, you can style your own, if you prefer."

"Ernie..." Hunter turned around in her chair to look directly at his face. "Where is Aggie?"

"She was here, but it's not a good day."

"Did she go home?"

"She's in the lounge. There was sudden, terrible pain in her arms and legs earlier. But… I had specific orders to make sure you get your hair done. You're live in twenty-two minutes." He seemed nervous.

"You're not going to lose your job, Ernie. Trust me. I'll save your ass. Now forget my hair. I need to see Aggie." The ends of her seafoam green robe swayed back and forth over her bare knees as she hurried out of there.

Aggie was lying down on the sofa in the lounge. One of the interns had brought her a paper cup of water from the studio's water cooler supplier, Honest Water. She was passionate about saving the environment and she had recently convinced upper management to cease buying cases of bottled water. Hunter could still hear Aggie's pitch line, *"It's reliable, purified drinking water at an affordable price. The owner himself delivers, and let me tell you, he's a sight for sore eyes."* Aggie was vibrant and persuasive and intelligent — and always so full of life. What was happening to her was heartbreaking for everyone who knew and loved her. Hunter saw that in spades right now with the expressions of those around them, backstage at the studio. *Worried. Sad. Sorrowful.*

"Hey, no resting on the job. My hair looks like shit," Hunter chose to channel their brand of shared humor, as she wiggled her way onto the edge of the sofa near Aggie's torso. She thumbed off the sweat beading from above her brow. "You okay?" She kept her voice low. Aggie absolutely hated drawing attention to herself. *What complete opposites those two were.*

"I had an episode. Muscle cramps in my arms and legs. I guess I'm tired and pushing myself this morning," she admitted. "But we had a wonderful weekend with the boys." Aggie's eyes beamed. *And Hunter momentarily pondered what in the world her boys were going to do without their mommy? One day.* "Remember how tough Mondays used to be for us after getting drunk all weekend?" Aggie attempted to laugh out loud at her recollection of the good ole days shared between them, but she coughed instead. After she paused to take a sip of water, Hunter heard her say, "This is tougher."

¥¥¥

Later, Hunter was trying to bat away the tears she held fiercely in her eyes as someone handed her the script, and told her she was on in three minutes. She had to focus on the interview ahead. She would, somehow, put out of her mind that Aggie wanted to talk to her after her segment. *Let's take a drive,* she suggested, *just the two of us,* and Hunter had actually laughed. Because she had a driver. It had been a few years since Hunter was behind the wheel of a car. Today, she would do that for Aggie.

"Sixty seconds, Hunter…" she heard in her ear monitor. It was time to forget all else for awhile.

¥¥¥

Ann Arbor, Michigan was a forty-five minute drive from downtown Detroit. That, Aggie told Hunter in the driver's seat of her own minivan, was their destination.

No one on Hunter's security team knew that she left the studio. That was not protocol. She reported her whereabouts to them at all times. Needless to say, both of their significant others were oblivious to the fact that they were headed down some of the most scenic roads in southeastern Michigan.

It felt liberating for Hunter to drive again. Only she rolled her eyes at the fact that she was behind the wheel of and navigating a minivan.

"So uncool. Really? Nothing blares 'mom' more than a freaking minivan."

"You'll find out one day that being a mom will be your greatest joy," Aggie told her, sincerely.

There were those two words, fused together, again. *One day.* It pained Hunter to think that Aggie would not be around to love on her first baby. She always thought Aggie would be a Godmother to her children, as Hunter was to both of Aggie's sons.

"I wish you could be here with me when I do become a mom. I want you to hold my baby, Ags."

Aggie turned to her from the passenger seat. "Get yourself pregnant then."

They laughed.

"After last night, I sure as hell could be," Hunter quipped.

"Do you love him?" Aggie asked, already able to see beaming happiness —and serenity— in her best friend's eyes that she had only seen one other time in her life. When she and Cooper were together.

"I do," Hunter smiled. "He's it for me. I can feel it."

"Amen." Aggie closed her eyes for a moment.

"You okay?"

"As okay as I can be knowing that God has only allocated me thirty-something years. I'm going to die. I'm leaving a life that I truly love."

Hunter was focused on driving the twists and turns of the route that hugged a portion of the Huron River. She heard Aggie's every word, and had the tears in her eyes to prove it. "I was doing some research on ALS, and you could live years, Ags."

"In pain and on the decline, yes, I could live a few more years, give or take," Aggie agreed. "But you understand that I won't deteriorate like that. I don't want to do that to my boys or to Jay."

Hunter nodded, and reached for Aggie's hand on her lap, and held it for a moment.

"So where are we headed? Just for a scenic drive? Or do you want to grab some lunch somewhere?"

"Grams lived in Ann Arbor, in that little two-story yellow house on big land, as she used to say."

"I remember," Hunter smiled.

"My cousin, Jamie bought all of it after Grams died. He was thirty years old then with a young family, and that was eighteen years ago."

"Is he still there?"

"He is," Aggie stated.

"I can't believe your grandma has been gone that long. I remember spending some fun summers with you out there on that land. Remember the little bridge over the pond? And the barn that was bigger than the house? We hung out in there for hours. I saw my first penis in there."

Aggie laughed out loud. "You did more than look at it!" They both remembered when Hunter went *all the way* in that barn with the farm boy down the lane road adjacent to Grams' place.

"Why there?" Hunter asked, turning serious again.

"You'll see," was all Aggie offered in response, and they drove on.

¥¥¥

The minivan bounced down the lane road. The place looked quiet. No vehicles. No activity on the grounds. Aggie told Hunter to drive up to the barn. When they reached it, Hunter parked directly in front of it. "It looks the same," Hunter noted from memory, and Aggie agreed.

"It sure does. The red paint is still chipping and peeling away in all the same places. Remember the sealed-off garage that Grams had in there? She would walk a mile from the house, in cold weather, to get to the barn and into that small heated garage where she parked 'her warm car,' she used to say."

"Too funny," Hunter grinned. "Wonder if it's still in there?"

"I'm counting on it to be," Aggie stated.

Hunter creased her brow. "What's going on in that head of yours?"

"Planning for the day when you drive me out here one last time."

"Oh Ags, no."

"Please. Just listen. I've been thinking a lot about how I will leave this world. I don't want to inflict anymore pain on myself. And I certainly don't want you to have to do anything that you cannot stomach. I know how queasy you get at the sight of blood."

"Can we please not do this now? Damn it, Ags."

"All I will ask is for you to drive me out here. And then you can call Jackson for your ride back."

Hunter felt the hot tears sting her eyes. She didn't know if she could. She would have to watch her start up the engine, or maybe even do it for her. And then, she would close the doors all around her. All the while, knowing she was taking in her last breaths. Alone. The tears were streaming off of Hunter's face now.

"You're not a crier," Aggie reminded her.

"Well this is fucking sad!" Hunter yelled at her. "And I'm mad. At you. I wanted to hold your hand through it. I don't know, I imagined you would take too many pills or something. And then I could lay by you for hours on end before I called for help."

Aggie shook her head no. "You would be implicating yourself, and I cannot die knowing that. But, I do appreciate the idea you imagined. It's peaceful in an odd way. I love you even more for it."

"Why carbon monoxide poisoning? Why out here at your Grams' home, of all places?"

"Because it was her idea," Aggie confessed, and Hunter's eyes widened.

"Are you telling me that you're seeing ghosts now?"

"No. She was alive, but dying. I rolled her wheelchair across that bridge overlooking her pond. We sat there together for awhile, not speaking, and then she told me she wished she had not let that awful disease take so much from her. And she knew there was more suffering to come. She said to me, 'Agatha Sue, if I still had my car, I would ask you to put me in it inside the barn and seal the doors until my last poisonous breath.'"

Hunter felt as if she couldn't catch her own breath right now. She silently damned the hardships of life and the unfairness of death forcing its untimely way in too soon in the lives of people like Aggie's grandmother who was only sixty-nine years old when she succumbed to disease — and then Cooper, and Kathryn. And now Aggie.

"You'll do it for me, won't you? Hunter, you're the only one who can."

Hunter turned to her. "I will. But it's going to kill me to walk away from you, knowing what I know, after doing what I've done."

"Good, then I'll see you on the other side much sooner than I expected," Aggie cracked a smile. And Hunter instantly fired back, in their language, "You're such a bitch."

Their arms were wrapped around each other in a tight embrace over the counsel between them. They held on for dear life, as if there was no tomorrow.

Chapter 24

The news story that flooded all of the local networks, and perhaps national too, was one that ABS NewsChannel 7 had assigned another reporter to cover. Cory Stark, who co-anchored the ABS early morning news, was live at Wayne County Jail in Detroit. Hunter watched the story on one of the television screens perched high on the studio wall. She already spoke to both Bash and Jay Marks on speaker phone in her office. They called her together as soon as they heard the news. Hunter had already known Jimmy Jenkins was killed by an inmate during the night. The cell guard was reported as temporarily distracted when the nineteen-year-old, with a pending trial and sentencing, was found strangled to death.

Hunter watched the latest ABS live news update from one of their own. She stood backstage in three-inch black heels, wearing a three-quarter-length sleeved, velvet black dress with a generous v-neckline, that ended just above the knee. She had her arms folded across her chest as she watched and listened. Each time she heard the story, she felt a wave of relief overcome her. There was a constant threat in the back of her mind, *What if he's freed one day and comes after me again?* She felt guilty for that as a part of her still believed he could have been reformed. Hunter saw something in his demeanor that day, just before he made the attempt to take his own life. Whatever that was, it sparked her drive to make a difference in a world full of troubled souls. The Coop remained front and center in her mind. And, soon, she would make it a reality.

"When are you going to let me have it?" Bruce walked up to her, sporting black suspenders with his black suit pants and white long-sleeved shirt.

"For not putting me on that story?" Bruce didn't react, so Hunter kept speaking. "I would be lying if I said I am not disappointed," she told him, "but I kept my mouth shut for once." He chuckled under his breath. "Why didn't you give me the story?"

"I believe we all have our limits, even the best and brightest in the business. The Jenkins name has done enough damage to you. It's time to find peace, and reporting his death on-air was not the way for you to do that. Give it a few days and this story will be dead and buried right with him."

Hunter was surprised at Bruce. He was a cut-throat business man, yes, but callous didn't suit him. "Bruce?" was all she said as she turned to look him directly in the eye.

"You are like a daughter to me, always have been, sweetheart. Seeing you in danger, right before my eyes in this studio, while I was standing here feeling like a useless fool, just did something to me. Let me tell you… that was a light-bulb moment for me… news isn't everything. There I said it," he smirked.

"But," Hunter was quick to offer her rebuttal, "it damn near is everything when you put your heart and soul into it the way you taught me. Look around you. No one has surpassed us in the ratings since you've been at the helm. This is quite a legacy you have built here, Bruce Rudis."

"Only you would say that to me at a time when I'm ready to hang up my tie."

"You don't wear a tie," she quipped, trying to make light of a truth that she was not ready to face.

"Right," he nodded with a lopsided grin on his face. "I have two very successful sons, and two smart, gorgeous daughters-in-law. They've all given me three grandchildren now. Those people are my real legacy. My wife thinks this is my most brilliant idea yet. We can travel the world. We can slow down and cherish the years we have left together."

Hunter felt teary. Life was full of change, and too damn many goodbyes. But this, she would make this, a happy moment for a man who took under his wing a rookie journalist, so green in the business, and molded her into a confident, successful career woman. Her need, her greater need, for him in her professional life, was crying out in defiance right now. "Don't say the R word, Bruce." She never thought she would see the day. Retirement was not a word logged in his vocabulary.

He chuckled. "Then I'll say the P word. I'm proud to walk away at the top of my game. And I'm so very proud of you. You're happy and fulfilled again, I can see it. You've turned a corner in your personal life that I was beginning to think wouldn't happen. Because you weren't allowing it." He momentarily held the side of her face with an open palm. "I want to turn on the news every single morning to see you taking this network to new heights. And I also want to be invited to your wedding, one day, and to all of those chaotic birthday parties as your babies grow. Balance is key, always remember that."

Hunter lunged herself into his arms. She cried this time. The once ambitious, young girl who proved herself to this news man, this seasoned production man, had grown to endlessly love and respect him. And, Bruce wouldn't merely be invited to her wedding. He would walk her down the aisle. And he would be like a grandpa to her babies. *One day.*

¥¥¥

After Jackson drove her home from the studio, Hunter sank onto her sofa. And back into an all-too-familiar groove of pain. She hadn't changed out of her black velvet dress. She only kicked off her heels and curled her bare feet underneath her, with a full glass of wine in her hand.

Jenkins was dead. That story was over. She allowed her relief to take over any lingering questions she had.

Aggie was dying. Gradually. Slowly, yet not that damn slow. She was not at the news studio again today, because she had a doctor's appointment with a different specialist. This one she was advised to see for limb onset. Most of her current symptoms of ALS had settled in as muscle weakness and atrophy. She texted Hunter following that appointment. They were just words on her phone screen, as she had not actually heard Aggie's voice, but the emotion in them spoke volumes.

I'm a special case, it seems. I may even go down in the world book of records. ALS is progressing in my body faster than even you can say FUCK.

Hunter didn't smile. Even their shared, weird humor couldn't change the seriousness of this disease. She knew that was why Aggie had chosen to text instead of call.

She was lost in alcohol again, by the time Bash arrived. Jay Marks had taken the night off to be with his wife. Jackson was filling in. She knew Bash had entered the gate, but she had not moved from the sofa to unlock the door. He knocked first anyway, so she got up.

Bash took one look at her when she opened the door, and he knew. This was an image of the woman he first met. Lost. Closed off. Sad, but pretending not to be. He stepped inside, and turned the deadbolt once he closed the door behind him. "I talked to Jay," was all he said. It was enough. He knew about Aggie, so Hunter didn't have to say it out loud.

She nodded, and drank until she finished the last of the wine in her glass. "I need a refill, be right back," she tipped her empty glass his way, and attempted to move. Bash caught her by the shoulders. "Let's wait on that," he suggested. "Sit down. We'll talk about how you're feeling instead of drowning it all in alcohol."

Hunter pulled away from him. "Don't judge me."

"I'm not. I just need for you to face this. You need to deal with this in a healthy way."

"Let's talk about need," she began, as if she was suddenly on a mission to be heard. "I have always been one to need the hell out of people. I fall in head first, I get attached, I feed that need with more of whoever I have in my life or whatever I'm doing. It's factual. It's who we are as people. In every relationship that exists, there is one person who has the greater need. It's a reality. I tend to hog that greater need every damn time. It's exhausting, and I'll tell you why..." Bash listened raptly. He stood close to her and he could smell the wine on her breath. She wasn't drunk. Not yet. And, as always, she spoke diligently and profoundly. "I'm tired. I've worn myself out. Because I always end up losing those people. That, my love, is painfully true." She set her empty wine glass down on a small table in the foyer and turned to walk away from him.

He followed her to the sofa. She plopped down on it, and he sat on the glass table directly in front of her. She looked surprised to see his large frame, and great-looking-ass in those tight jeans, somehow fit on that tabletop space in front of her.

"I've shared very little with you about Kathryn," Bash began, and he all at once had Hunter's attention. It's not that she wanted to know more about the woman he was married to, but she was curious what Bash had to say. "I told you that she was a pediatric nurse. Successful. Smart. Caring. We grew and changed together in our relationship after being married for almost three years. There were things I just did, because I knew she needed me to do them. I cooked dinner because she worked longer hours in the evening than I did at that time. I did the dishes because she was tired and wanted to soak in the bath. I did my own laundry because she always turned my white shirts pink. I took care of all of our yardwork. I was the cheap handyman in our fixer-upper house. I knew how to change the oil and rotate the tires on our vehicles," Bash paused. "I could keep going and list all the things that I did for her, and for us. Because I wanted to. And because Kathryn needed me to." Hunter couldn't help but see Bash as one of those nice guys who didn't deserve a woman who took advantage of him. But when Bash spoke again, she instantly regretted her hasty assumption.

"When Kathryn was sixteen, she lost her leg in a motorcycle accident. She had been riding behind her boyfriend on a Gold Wing. It was his father's large bike, and he was too young and inexperienced to be handling it. They crashed, and her leg was severed at the accident scene. When I met Kathryn many years later, she was a confident prosthetic wearer. I never just saw her handicap. There was so much more to her. But I always felt a great need to take care of her. And she allowed me to. She depended on me. And yes, I think over time she had the greater need in our relationship, as you spoke of. When I lost her, I lost a piece of myself. I no longer had a purpose. My reason to get up and get things accomplished was gone. There was no one there to take care of anymore. Until you came along."

Hunter was caught off guard by everything he was telling her, and especially his last comment regarding her. She was anything but needy when it came to men. That, at least, was how she perceived herself after she lost Cooper. She never wanted to become so dependent on a man's love that she lost herself if he were to ever leave. There were infinite times when it hurt to just breathe without Cooper in her life.

"When we first met, I saw a woman who physically needed protection. I was drawn to the idea of keeping you safe, professionally. But then I saw past that strong, independent, I-don't-need-anyone-else persona that you put up around yourself like barriers. I fell in love with your vulnerability that you show to very few people. You are quick to label yourself as someone who always consumes the greater need. I don't see that with us. I don't feel that from you."

Hunter looked down at her bare feet, which were almost toe-to-toe with Bash's boots on the floor. That's because, with Bash, it was different. Everything felt equal. The give and take didn't weigh heavier on her end or his. It was in sync. They were in sync. But one of her greatest fears with her commitment to him was, *What if they ever lost that? What if they became too comfortable sharing life and one day she would find herself needing him more?* To Hunter, that was the cruel cycle she had lived for most of her life. As far back as she could remember as a child, she needed her parents to be there for her emotionally, but their careers always came first. And when she was eleven years old, she met Aggie. Aggie continued to be her only constant in life. Cooper came and went in the most heartbreaking way. And then Bash entered her world and put the broken pieces of her heart back together.

"And I like it," Bash continued to explain. "I like needing you so much that it hurts. I have the greatest need in the world to have you by my side. I'm not ashamed to say that feeling is a complete one-eighty for me. I need you. I feel needed by you, too. But there are moments, like this, when I feel you backing away from me. It's what you do when you are done with the hurt that life hurdles at you. It doesn't have to be that way for you anymore. Let me share some of that load. I can carry a lot on these big shoulders." Bash purposely straightened his posture and puffed out his chest.

Hunter smiled at him through the tears in her eyes that suddenly welled up and threatened to break free. "There aren't too many people in my life who can read me the way you can."

"Good," Bash said, placing his entire hand over one of her bare knees that were nearly touching with his own.

"If I asked you for something, would you make it happen?" Hunter was bold and brave, and most times she went with her gut-feeling. *Just say it, or do it. Rethink it later.* That was Hunter's lifelong motto.

"Absolutely. Anything at all." He loved her unconditionally.

"Do life with me," she began. Bash grinned and chuckled a little, as he waited for Hunter to completely clarify where she was going with this. "Marry me. Have babies with me."

He didn't say a word in answer. This was the act-on-impulse woman he loved. *Just feel. Just be.* He only pulled her close and met her lips with his own. She kissed him in return, desperately and with their familiar mounting passion. And when he pulled back, his voice was raspy. "I know you want to wear the pants in this relationship," he teased in reference to everything they spoke of, "but that request, that marriage proposal is kind of my job." She giggled, and he continued to be silly with her, "So do you have a ring for me to show all of my friends?" She laughed out loud. "And about those baby daddy demands… we should go upstairs and work on that right now, don't you think?" Hunter moved her body onto his lap. She disregarded the fact that she was wearing a dress which already shifted above her hips. He groaned when she straddled him. "One more thing…" he started to add, and Hunter's full attention was on him. "You bring just the right amount of naughty into my life."

"Good girls are boring," she whispered into his ear.

Chapter 25

Six weeks later, Hunter managed to locate and rent a 1968 blue Dodge Polara convertible. The body of it was every bit of the old classic like Grams owned, but the entire engine of this car was updated. She completed the paperwork in Aggie's name, and then paid cash for the car rental fee. It was an exact replica of the car that Hunter remembered from many years ago. She and Aggie were teenagers, giggling at Grams when she put the top down and sped off on her dusty lane road. It was as if she was trying to capture her youth again with the wind in her hair.

Aggie was using a three-pronged cane now to help her walk. She was in constant pain, as the muscles in her legs were cramping from the degeneration. She was losing weight as she couldn't swallow food without a struggle. She still had her voice. Thankfully, the stuttering had come and gone almost overnight. She was still able to express how much she loved her husband and her little boys. And she had told them so one last time. Jay Marks had sensed what was happening in the most overwhelming way, but he never questioned his wife. *Her choice had been made.*

He witnessed her struggle to make her legs bend down to the floor where their children were playing and entirely oblivious to how final this moment in time would be. She pressed her lips to the top of their heads, one by one, and inhaled the scent of their hair. *Of her little boys.* They were the part of her that she would leave behind in this world.

When Hunter arrived, and Aggie saw that classic convertible parked on the driveway, she appreciated the instant wave of peace that it brought her. "You are the most amazing soul. Thank you," she whispered in Hunter's ear as they stood on the front porch of her home that she shared with Jay and their boys. It was a new, colonial-style house that they had built just two years ago. Her most favorite part of that house, inside and out, was the wrap-around front porch. There were two, high-back rocking chairs placed off to the side of the front door. *She was supposed to grow old in one of those rockers.*

Both Jay and Hunter assisted Aggie to the car. The cane was useless to her now. Hunter heard Jay choking on tears as he held his wife in his arms one last time. Hunter looked down and stepped away from them as they exchanged words of affection and goodbyes.

She waited on the bottom step of the porch after she sat down. She needed all of her strength today. She already felt shaky, as her nerves had gotten the best of her.

Jay Marks eventually walked over to her. His eyes were red, and the tears were dripping off his clean-shaven face. He sat down two steps above Hunter. She stood, and turned around to face him. His elbows were on his quads as he hung his headlow. Hunter leaned forward and pressed her lips to his bald head. He reached his arms completely around her waist and held on. She held him back tightly, and then strengthened her grip, as he tried his damnedest to muffle his sobs. Aggie watched the heartbreaking scene from the passenger seat of the car.

¥¥¥

Hunter drove them to Ann Arbor, with the convertible top down. They spoke very little, and most times when Hunter glanced at Aggie she had her eyes closed and wore a serene smile on her face. The wind in her hair made her happy in the moment. And that was all that mattered to Hunter right now. She was going to take this moment by moment. She was struggling, as she still had yet to feel it in her soul that this was the right thing to do.

When they reached Aggie's grandmother's old farmhouse and the land that housed the barn, Hunter parked the convertible close to that old barn. She never moved to open any doors, or to pull the vehicle inside. Aggie had to be certain of what she was doing before Hunter helped her do anything further.

"No one is home, but the barn will be unlocked. I called Jamie ahead. He thinks I just want to look around, for old time's sake. He said he doesn't use the barn much, but the closed-off space that Grams used as a garage is still in there."

"Well you certainly did your homework," Hunter stated as if this was just a typical day and another conversation shared between them. Aggie recognized the barriers she had put up around herself. To protect herself from the overwhelming pain.

"I want you to always remember something," Aggie spoke, and Hunter fought the lump rising from her chest to her throat. "Don't hate yourself for this. It's what I want. Remind yourself of that. Over and over. I am no longer going to be in pain. You're saving me from that, and especially from losing myself deeper and deeper into this horrific decline."

Hunter nodded her head, and wouldn't make eye contact with Aggie. "I'm scared," she finally said, and Aggie reached for her hand. "I'm scared of where you're going. Can you somehow let me know that you arrived safely?"

Aggie reacted with a giggle, which sounded more like a snort. "Sure, I'll text you."

"I mean it," Hunter was adamant. She was going to need a sign from her. "I don't know, come back, like they say, as a butterfly or a bird. Don't shit on me though. Just bring me some peace, will you?"

"I will move heaven and earth to get that message back to you." Aggie let a few tears trickled down her cheeks. "Love on my boys for me, okay? Make sure they pick good women someday. Be my voice when they need it. And Jay… keep him busy. He doesn't do well with time on his hands. And when he wants to move on with someone else, don't be a bitch about it." They laughed a little, as their hands were still clenched on the front seat of that classic convertible.

"I love you, Ags," Hunter managed to choke out the words, and force back her tears.

"I've always loved you the most, you know that," Aggie declared.

Hunter turned to her. She kissed her forehead that was beading with sweat. Aggie closed her eyes for a moment.

"Are you absolutely sure about this? Because if you have one inkling of doubt, I will turn this car around faster than Grams on the way to the flea market."

Aggie smiled. "What I love most about you is no matter the amount of doubt that you're carrying in your heart right now, you are asking me to admit mine. You are strong and you are brave. I knew you could put me first in my greatest time of need."

"Your level of selfishness has always been off the charts," Hunter quipped. But, her knees were shaking and her hands were trembling. Her life had not always been easy thus far, but this was going to go down as the hardest thing she ever had to do. And yes, she had to do it. For Agatha Sue, the eleven-year-old girl who could always see her soul. And vice versa.

¥¥¥

The car was backed into the enclosed garage, located on the far side of the barn. The garage door, which Hunter had to raise by hand, faced the back of the building. It remained open as they sat together in shared silence.

"From what I read, all you have to do is breathe... and you'll just drift off to sleep." Hunter spoke of this as if it were just another topic she had researched for a story.

"Easy enough," Aggie replied.

"But there's never been an easy goodbye between us," Hunter said, forcing Aggie to give her direct eye contact. She wanted to see those blue eyes behind those dark-rimmed glasses one more time, so she could freeze that image in her

mind. *Not that she could ever forget her face.* "There's always one more word to say, one more hug to squeeze out of each other. I'm not going to make the first move here. You know I can't. Push me out of this car when you are ready. Tell me to just go. Make me, Ags. I can't do this by myself."

"I'll wait until you pull down the garage door completely... before I start the engine," Aggie said, still looking into Hunter's eyes.

"A part of me wants to stay here with you." Hunter's honesty was frightening, even for her to hear herself say.

"Don't you dare. You have a wonderful life with Bash ahead of you, and beautiful babies to make. Not to mention that the world needs your talent in front of that camera. You are going to be old and wrinkly when I welcome you at the entry gate to heaven. Finally, I'll be the beautiful one with better posture!" Aggie's laugh echoed in that old garage.

"Be serious," Hunter reprimanded her. "I think I do want to look at us that way. A part of me will go with you, just like a part of you will stay with me. We'll always be somewhere inside each other. In the way that we sass. In how deeply we love, because you were the first person I ever loved without boundaries. You taught me love's worth."

"I could say all the same about you," Aggie inhaled one last, long deep breath of the fresh air blowing into the barn. "Go on, Hunter. I'm ready."

Chapter 26

She didn't know for certain how much time had passed. It felt like an eternity as Hunter sat on the little bridge with her knees pulled up to her chest. The pond water underneath rippled from the wind. She sobbed until she choked on her own tears. She shook her fist at the heavens, expressing her disapproval of this fate. What precisely was God's will anyway? And how could he ever have an acceptable explanation for taking Aggie away from all of them? Especially her little boys.

Finally, she texted Jackson the address and told him to come pick her up. It seemed like no time at all had passed, only minutes, when she heard a car turn onto the lane road. As far as Hunter could tell, it wasn't the full-size SUV that Jackson drove. She wondered if it was Aggie's cousin, Jamie. And then she recognized Bash's car.

Hunter wasn't prepared for this. All she had planned for was a no-questions-asked drive with Jackson, back to Detroit to her estate. Aggie's wish was for Jamie to find her. She believed it would be less emotional that way. *Poor Cousin Jamie.* Hunter then would not be directly connected to the tragedy.

Bash got out of his car, and slowly made his way toward her. He didn't have the words this time. He wasn't entirely sure if he fully supported what those two women did out there on that once fertile farmland.

When he reached Hunter, he didn't have to say anything after all. She fell into his arms. "Just hold me. Please. Hold. Me." She cried until she was spent in his arms. And then she realized that Bash deserved to know what happened.

"You're going to judge me, and you're going to be angry with Aggie," she spoke, as her face was makeup-free and wet with tears.

"There's no need for you to explain. I already know. And, like Jay, I am in complete awe of your courage." Hunter wanted to cry again. She didn't feel brave or bold right now. She, in fact, had never felt more helpless or useless as she sat on the weathered, broken wooden planks of that bridge and did absolutely nothing while her best friend took her own life, just a matter of yards away from her. The pit of Hunter's stomach hurt. She struggled to breathe, thinking of Aggie's final breaths inside of that barn.

"I need your help," she said to Bash, and he listened. "Ags wanted her cousin who lives here to find her. She didn't want to put that on me. But I want to get her out of there. I just don't know if I can do it alone, or at all. Bash, please..."

"He took ahold of her hands. He faced her. "I want you to stay here, or stay back. Maybe get into my car. I will go to her."

Hunter didn't object. She stayed, on the bridge still, while Bash made his way over to the barn. On the walk there, Bash rehashed in his mind what he had known about the scene of carbon monoxide poisoning. It only took minutes in a sealed space for carbon monoxide to build up in a person's bloodstream. When the concentration of the toxic gas in the air increases and the lungs begin to pull it in, a body will start to replace oxygen with it. The results are unconsciousness and, quickly thereafter, death.

Bash stretched his t-shirt upward by the neck opening, and he covered his mouth and nose. He kept his face inside his shirt when he reached the closed garage door and bent his knees to lift it with both of his hands. The moment the door was raised, he was taken aback. While he was well aware that the gas was colorless and odorless, he didn't expect the scene that he found in there.

It felt like it was taking Bash too long, and Hunter began pacing the planks on that bridge. She folded her arms across her chest. She was sad and she felt lost, but she never sensed that Aggie was gone. That emptiness had yet to hit her, she assumed. Or, as they had spoken about in Aggie's final moments on this earth, perhaps it truly was possible for them to always be a part of each other.

Her thoughts were interrupted when she heard Bash call her name. She looked at him from afar. He was standing at a corner of the barn, opposite from where Hunter had left Aggie in that car. He frantically waved her over there with his entire arm in the air. At first Hunter shook her head no. And then, something forced her to rush toward him. She was within a few feet of Bash when she heard him say, "Someone wants to see you."

Life, a second chance at it, or something else extremely powerful, flooded her entire being as Bash spoke those words to her. Hunter didn't question him, or how in the world Aggie could still be alive and asking for her. She reacted and ran past him, as he followed on her heels.

When she reached the open garage, Hunter saw Aggie, sitting in the passenger seat of that convertible. She still had life pumping through her body. Again, Hunter never spoke. She rushed to her and held her and kissed her face over and over. Bash watched the two of them, with tears in his eyes. This, no matter how long Aggie would live, was a second chance.

"I thought you were—"

"I forgot one important thing that Grams told me so long ago," Aggie stopped Hunter from speaking and her words instantly forced her to listen. "She wished she had taken her own life before she lost her dignity, yes, but then she said, *'It was in God's hands.'*"

Hunter lunged toward her and held her again. "Oh Ags… you changed your mind. I'll never forget how grateful I feel right now to have you back. I thought I had lost you. I was sitting out there on that bridge, crying my eyes out, and wondering what was happening to you." Hunter pondered now if Aggie even closed the convertible top or started the engine.

"Nothing like you were thinking," Aggie explained. "I just sat here, overwhelmed with how close I came to ending my own life. And then I started thinking about what I do have. I realized these eyes of mine can still see, and my ears can still hear, and my heart can still love. I want to utilize what I have left of me until the very end. I want to take in all that I can of my boys while I am still here with them. I guess you could say I had a change of heart. My need to be here —for as long as I possibly can— is greater than this illness or my pride or whatever else clouded my judgement in my desperate moments."

Hunter understood. Clearly, this was about having a greater need.

Epilogue

"Hunter, you're on in five..." The voice in her ear monitor was not the familiar, appeasing one of Bruce Rudis. And her platinum blonde hair was cut into a shorter, angular bob that she had styled herself this morning. She chose to do that sometimes. Some days were less tough than others as she sifted through the changes in her life.

It had been two years since Aggie left this world behind. She lived an additional ten and half months following that fateful day when she *changed her mind.* Hunter would forever be grateful for their gift of time for many reasons — but especially because Aggie had been able to meet Hunter and Bash's baby girl. Three days following her birth, Aggie died from ALS. When one adored soul left this earth, another had arrived. It was the circle of life. And it was the most bittersweet thing that Hunter had ever experienced.

"Good morning, Detroit. I'm Hunter Perry," she smiled into the camera. She was happy and fulfilled being married to Sebastian Perry. She was also overwhelmingly sad at times, living her life without Aggie. She chose to focus on the things that brought her joy, and this story today was special to her.

"Yesterday, I prerecorded a segment that we are going to air right now. In celebration of the one-year grand opening of The Coop, we are giving you, the viewers, a special peek inside."

"You're back on in exactly three and half minutes," the new producer of ABS NewsChannel 7 spoke in her ear. The funny thing is, the forty-something man was not *new* to the network after having already replaced Bruce a year and a half ago. But someone else in Bruce's place would always be *new and different* to Hunter. And this guy always wore a tie.

Hunter's assistant joined her on set for a moment as the segment at The Coop was running, on air, on ABS, for another couple of minutes.

"Daycare called," she spoke quickly to Hunter. "Someone isn't feeling well this morning. They want you to pick her up as soon as possible."

"Oh no." Aggie Sue had not slept well for Hunter and Bash last night. Hunter suspected her ears were bothering her again, and she had chest congestion too. "I need a phone." Her assistant handed Hunter her own cell phone. She stepped off to the side. He answered on the second ring. "Bash, it's me. Our baby girl is sick and I'm live in only one minute. Will you pick her up and I'll meet you both at home as soon as I can?"

Bash was now a detective for the Detroit Police Department. He and Jay Marks both were now on the force together. *Brothers in blue.* Jackson was making money these days on the streets of Michigan as an uber driver.

"I will do that. I really hate when she's sick." In Hunter's heart, that man snagged *Daddy of the Year* since the day Aggie Sue was born.

"Thank you. Me too, honey. Call you later. I gotta go!"

¥¥¥

Hunter punched in the code at the gate outside of her estate. That was the only defense she had now. The cameras, her security team, and a driver were no longer necessities. She drove up to the circle drive and spotted the loves of her life on the front porch. Bash was in plain clothes, with his police badge clipped onto the belt loop of his denim. He sat on one of the rocking chairs that Jay Marks had given them when he and the boys moved into a smaller house that had no extra space for those chairs Aggie loved so much. He wanted Hunter to have them. In Bash's arms was a sleepy little girl.

Hunter made her way up the porch steps. "How's my baby?" she pressed her lips to Aggie Sue's little forehead that felt clammy and heated. Her dark hair, like her daddy's —and like her namesake, Hunter chose to believe— was matted on the far sides of her rosy cheeks.

"The pediatrician prescribed an antibiotic to help those little ears feel better fast," Bash said, as he cradled her.

The sight of the two of them together, their baby in her husband's arms, was one that she could stare at for hours. Hunter sat down on the rocking chair next to theirs. "Oh I hope so," she said in reference to feeling better. "Mommy doesn't feel the best either."

Bash turned to look at her. "What hurts?"

"Oh nothing hurts. Just this feeling that I'm going to have to tolerate for the next nine months..."

Bash's face lit up. "Are you serious?"

Hunter smiled wide and repeatedly nodded her head.

"Here we go, Aggie Sue. Get ready to listen to mommy whine for wine every night because she can't have it..."

"Stop. You're being ridiculous," Hunter playfully rolled her eyes, and then she recalled that torturous sacrifice. "Was I really *that* bad?"

"Worse than you can possibly imagine," Bash kidded her with a wink.

"This is your fault, you know? If you would just keep your hands to yourself."

"Oh I know," Bash agreed with her. "My need is greater."

Hunter laughed, and she was quick to admit, "I'm not so sure about that anymore."

About the Author

In every relationship, someone always has the greater need. It's reality. And not at all a bad thing. That concept alone was the true inspiration behind this book, my 20th published novel! It's always emotions and relationships and words of wisdom that I've heard or overheard along the way that enables me to keep doing this. I write because I fully enjoy it — and I want to share with all of you these stories that cycle through my mind (and my heart). One of my loyal readers once told me that I have "keyboard courage," and I laughed. And then she sincerely said that I have a way with creating characters that 'feel' how we all feel, and 'say' the things all of us wish we had the courage to convey. I do strive to awaken the emotions that most of us tuck away. And I hope I never lose the ability to reach all of you through fictional characters that truly are just like you and me.

As always, thank you for reading!

Love,

Lori Bell

Made in the USA
Middletown, DE
21 February 2019